柴田元幸ハイブ・リット

柴田元幸 編・訳
Barry Yourgrau
Rebecca Brown
Kelly Link
Stuart Dybek
Steven Millhauser
Paul Auster

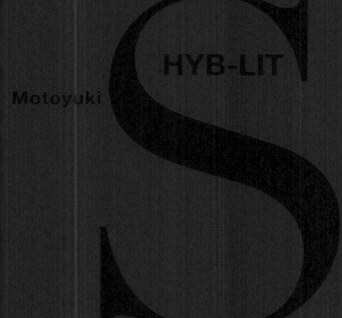

HYB-LIT

Motoyuki Shibata

アルク

Motoyuki Shibata Hyb-Lit
柴田元幸ハイブ・リット

柴田元幸 編・訳

Barry Yourgrau
Rebecca Brown
Kelly Link
Stuart Dybek
Steven Millhauser
Paul Auster

装幀　松田行正＋杉本聖士

Contents　目次

編訳者まえがき　柴田元幸 … 004
英語と文学を楽しむ『新装版　柴田元幸ハイブ・リット』　編集部編 … 010
音声の活用方法　編集部編 … 012

[Story 1] 🎧002-010
HAPPY BIRTHDAY by Barry Yourgrau
ハッピー・バースデイ／バリー・ユアグロー … 013

[Story 2] 🎧011-060
FOLIE A DEUX by Rebecca Brown
私たちがやったこと／レベッカ・ブラウン … 021

[Story 3] 🎧061-107
THE GREAT DIVORCE by Kelly Link
大いなる離婚／ケリー・リンク … 067

[Story 4] 🎧108-122
PET MILK by Stuart Dybek
ペット・ミルク／スチュアート・ダイベック … 111

[Story 5] 🎧123-138
SNOWMEN by Steven Millhauser
雪人間／スティーヴン・ミルハウザー … 129

[Story 6] 🎧139-164
AUGGIE WREN'S CHRISTMAS STORY by Paul Auster
オーギー・レンのクリスマス・ストーリー／ポール・オースター … 155

著者・訳者紹介 … 182
初出一覧・コピーライト … 183

小説を「聴く」こと

　この本の最大の「売り」は、何と言っても、すべて著者自身が読んだ、六本の短篇小説の朗読CDである。作者がそれぞれ自分の代表的な短篇を読んだCD、というのは英語圏でもそうざらにはないと思う。
　……と、なんだか、有難さの押し売りみたいな書き出しになってしまったので、急いで付け足しておくと、僕はべつに、小説を（たとえ作者自身による朗読であれ）「聴く」ことの方が、紙の上の文字を「読む」ことよりも、体験として格が上だとは思っていない。
　たとえば、これはほかのところでも書いたことだが、僕の訳している作家のなかでも、T・R・ピアソンなどは、文章自体は暇なおっさんが変てこな話をえんえん語っている感じを彷彿とさせるにもかかわらず、朗読は自分でするのも他人のを聴くのも好きではないと言っている。シェークスピアが朗読しに来ると言われても行く気はないね、と初めて会ったときに言っていた。
　もちろん、朗読嫌いでも、新刊が出れば朗読ツアーに送り出されるのがアメリカでは普通であり、ピアソン氏の朗読ビデオなどもちゃんと残っている。見せてもらったら、いやほんと、全然楽しくなさそうにものすごい早口で読んでいて、「あーっさっさと終わらせてトイレに行きてぇ」と思っているみたいな顔をしていた。
　そもそも、2時間の作品であれば2時間で観るしかない映画とは違って、文章の場合、1ページを1分で読むこともできれば、5分かけてじっくり読むのも自由である。たしかにビデオやDVDになって、あるシーンをもう一度観たりすることも可能になったが、10秒のシーンは依然

として10秒で観るしかないわけで、読むスピードが読者に委ねられている文章とはやはり違う。

　それにまた、たとえば登場人物の声にしても、文章ならそこからどのような声を想像しようと自由だが、映画ではとにかくもう物理的に声を与えられてしまい、想像の余地はない。

　要するに、文章というのは、受け手が実に多くをカスタマイズできる媒体なのである（もちろん、たとえ同じ映画を観ていても、結果的に観ているものは一人ひとり違うことは確かだけれども）。朗読を聴くというのは、だからある意味では、そういう文章の自由さを、すべて放棄することとも言える。そんなことやりたくないね、というピアソンのような人がいても、実は少しも不思議はないのである。

　とはいえ、物は言いよう、見ようであって、これとは全然違う見方をすることもできる。たとえば、一人で文章を読むことを、楽譜を読むことになぞらえてみよう。一通り音楽の知識があれば、我々は紙の上のオタマジャクシの並びを見て、頭のなかで音楽を作り出すことができる。『ゴルトベルク変奏曲』の楽譜を見て、リヒターふうの鬼気迫るチェンバロの演奏を「再生」することもできれば、グールドふうのマニエリスティックなピアノ演奏を脳内に響かせることもできる。

　これに対し、作家の朗読CDを聴くのは、まさにリヒターやグールドのCDを聴くことにあたるだろう。それによって、我々はたしかに多くの自由を放棄する。リヒターはもはやリヒターでしかありえないし、グールドについても、ほかの誰についてもしかり。

とはいえ、実際にCDで演奏を聴くことには、単に楽譜を「黙読」することでは得られない快楽があることを否定する人はほとんどいないだろう（もちろん、絶対いないとは言わない。というかむしろ、そういう人がいたら、ぜひ会って、その人が楽譜を読むときに脳内でどういうことが起きているのか、ぜひ訊いてみたい）。それと同じで、作家の朗読を聴くことには、声も限定され、スピードも限定されても、そうした限定を補って余りある直接性、生々しさがある。べつに年がら年中そういう生々しさに触れている必要はないが、時おりそういうものに触れ、自分の読み方、聴き方の外に出てみるのは、決して悪いことではないと思う。
　しかも、このCDブックは――と、また手前味噌に戻ってしまいますが――現代アメリカでも有数のすぐれた作家たちが、自分の代表作を読んでいて、いわば一流の音楽家が一堂に会してそれぞれ得意な曲を一曲ずつ弾いているような、実に贅沢な構成になっている。バリー・ユアグローの芝居っ気たっぷりのパフォーマンス。レベッカ・ブラウンの静謐な声に聞き取れる、ほんの少し怯えているような魅力的な震え。ケリー・リンクの、コミカルな内容をあくまでさりげなく読むことから生じるおかしさ。スチュアート・ダイベックの声の、いかにもシカゴ南部ふうに荒削りな、けれど驚くほど温かい響き。スティーヴン・ミルハウザーの、この人が肉声を持っていること自体ひとつの驚きなのに、実は朗読のお手本のように過不足なくドラマチックな読み方。そしてポール・オースターの、スモーカーらしくカッコよくしゃがれた声。どれをとっても、何度もくり返し聴くに値する朗読である。

もちろんこのCDをどのように聴こうと自由だが、もしかしたら、活字を追いながら聴くのはそんなに得策でないかもしれない。そういう聴き方は、往々にして、声を十分味わうことなく、活字を確認するだけで終わってしまうからである。それよりむしろ、まず活字を読んである程度内容も単語も頭に入れてから、目をつぶってじっくり聴く方が作品世界に深く入れるように思う（もちろん、英語力に自信のある方は、活字を読まずにまず耳から入っていいと思う —— まあそういうレベルの人には何もアドバイスは要りませんよね）。

　たとえばニュースなどのCDは、2度や3度聴くぶんにはとても勉強になるだろうが、一般的に言って、さすがに10回も20回も聴くのはなかなか辛いと思う。でも、すぐれた文学作品は、何度読んでも、何度聴いても面白いし、新しい発見がある。文学ほど、楽しむことと学ぶことが不可分に結びついている素材はほかにない。ぜひくり返し、内容が全部頭に入ってしまうくらい聴いていただければと思う。このCDブックが、多くの方々にとって、心地よい眠りへの格好の導き手になったり、鬱陶しい通勤電車を少しでも鬱陶しくないものにしてくれるなら、編者としては大変嬉しい。そしてその気持ちは、この本の企画からはじまって、版権交渉、録音の手配、注の作成、等々すべてにかかわってくださった、アルク英語事業部の白川雅敏さんも同じだと思う。

2008年10月
柴田元幸

新装版のためのまえがき

　2008年に出したこの本を復刊することができて、とても嬉しい。6人の作家が自作を朗読した音声とそのテクストを収めた本、というのはまだ他に例がない。——いや、あってもいいのだが、とにかくこの6短篇、どれも素晴らしく、聞きごたえ読みごたえがあるので、新しい読者の耳と目に届くことになって素直に嬉しい。

　全体的な前口上は「編訳者まえがき」に書いたので、ここでは作者6人の2008年以降の近況を伝えておく。

　バリー・ユアグローは2010年にハードボイルドのパロディ集『真夜中のギャングたち』邦訳が出た。現在は何度かの来日体験に基づき東京を舞台とする『オヤジギャグの華』を雑誌『波』に連載中。

　レベッカ・ブラウンは2009年に私的アメリカ文化論 *American Romances* を、2018年にはおとぎ話の語り直しを主とする作品集 *Not Heaven, Somewhere Else* を発表。2017年に4度目の来日、合わせて『かつらの合っていない女』が刊行された。

　ケリー・リンクは2016年に短篇集 *Get in Trouble* を発表、邦訳は2014年に『プリティ・モンスターズ』が出た。出版社 Small Beer Press の経営も続けている上に、2019年10月、地元マサチューセッツ州イーストハンプトンで書店を開いた。

　スチュアート・ダイベックは2014年に *Paper Lantern: Love Stories* と *Ecstatic Cahoots: Fifty Short Stories* の短篇集2冊を同時刊行。日本では第一短篇集（原書1980年刊）『路地裏の子供たち』の邦訳が2019年に出た。

　スティーヴン・ミルハウザーは2016年に初来日し、多くの読者をそ

の誠実な人柄で魅了した。2008年以降に出た邦訳は『魔法の夜』『木に登る王』『十三の物語』『私たち異者は』。

　ポール・オースターは2017年に900ページ近い大作4 3 2 1を刊行し話題に。近年の邦訳は『闇の中の男』『インヴィジブル』『冬の日誌』『内面からの報告書』など。

　以上、どの作家も依然として素晴らしい作品を生み出しつづけている。本書の6作を聞いて／読んで気に入った作家がいたら、ぜひ他作品もお読みいただければと思う。が、もちろん、まずはこの本を楽しんでいただけますように。

2019年11月
柴田元幸

英語と文学を楽しむ『柴田元幸ハイブ・リット』
編集部編／柴田元幸監修

　本書『柴田元幸ハイブ・リット』のタイトルにある「ハイブ・リット」とは、hybrid（混成の）と literature（文学）の合成語です。アメリカ短篇小説という「文学」を、❶原文、❷翻訳、❸朗読、といろいろな角度から味わうことで英語が学べる本シリーズの呼称です。ここでは、「ハイブ・リット」で英語力をアップさせる方法を目的別にお教えします。

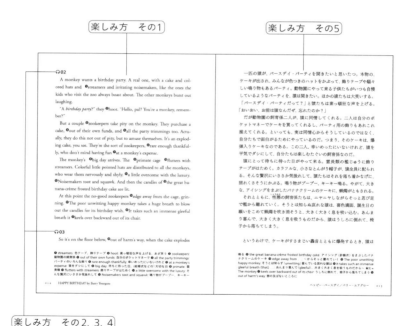

[楽しみ方　その1]
リーディング：物語を英語で読む
左ページには原文の英語を掲載しています。英語で小説を読んだことのない人も、右ページの訳やページ下の脚注を頼りに英語のリーディングに挑戦してみましょう。本書掲載の"Folie à Deux"や"Auggie Wren's Christmas Story"は比較的平易な英語で書かれているので、読みやすく感じるはずです。自信がついたら、それぞれの短篇を収録した原書に挑戦してみては？

[楽しみ方　その2]
リスニング：物語の朗読を聞く
本書には、作家自身による英語の朗読を用意しています。意味の固まりを意識しながら聞くと、英語の構文の感覚を養えるでしょう。何度も繰り返し聞くことで、英語のリズムやイントネーションに慣れ、リスニング力がアップします。

[楽しみ方　その3]
リピーティング：朗読を聴いて繰り返し言ってみる
リピーティングとは1センテンスごとに音声を止め、聞こえたままにまねをして、感情を込めて英語を口に出すことです。最初から全部をリピーティングするのではなく、お気に入りのパラグラフ（段落）を選んで取り組むとよいでしょう。英語をしっかりと聞き取ることでリスニング力、そして、忠実に再生することで話し方のリズムやイントネーションを身に付けられるのでスピーキング力アップに役立ちます。

[楽しみ方　その4]
ディクテーション：朗読の英語を書き取る
朗読の音声を繰り返し聞いて、英語を書き取ります。聞いて書き取ることによって現在の英語力を認識することができます。集中して英語を聞くのでリスニング力が伸び、英語が頭に残るのでスピーキングにも活きてきます。リピーティング同様、覚えてしまいたいくらいに気に入った1パラグラフから始めるのがよいでしょう。

[楽しみ方　その5]
トランスレーション：物語を日本語に訳す
翻訳はすべて柴田元幸によるものです。対訳形式なので、翻訳者がいかに英語を日本語に置き換えているかを読み比べることが可能です。物語を翻訳し、自訳と柴田訳とを較べて添削することによって、より深く英語のニュアンスを理解し味わうことができます。

【無料】英文音声の入手・活用方法　編集部編

本書の英文音声は、以下の要領で無料でダウンロードしていただけます。
本サービスのご利用には、メールアドレスIDの登録／ログインが必要となります（無料）。あらかじめご了承ください。

パソコンの場合

パソコンで、音声データをダウンロードするには、以下のURLから行います。

1）アルクのダウンロードセンター
　https://www.alc.co.jp/dl/
2）ログイン後、ダウンロードセンターで、書籍名または商品コード 7019059 でコンテンツを検索します。
3）検索後、ダウンロード用ボタンをクリックし、以下のパスワードを入力してコンテンツをダウンロードしてください。

スマートフォンの場合

スマートフォンまたはiPadに直接ダウンロードするには、無料アプリ「語学のオトモ ALCO」が必要です（ALCOインストール済みの方は3から）。iOS、Androidの両方に対応しています。再生スピードの変更や、秒数指定の巻き戻し・早送りなど、便利な機能が満載です。語学学習にぜひご活用ください。

1）ALCOのインストール
　https://www.alc.co.jp/alco/
2）インストール後、ALCOへのログインには、メールアドレスIDの登録が必要となります（無料）。
3）ALCOにログインし、ホーム画面の下部にある「ダウンロードセンター」バーをタップします（QRコードを使えば、以下4、5の操作が不要です）。
4）ダウンロードセンターで、書籍名または商品コード 7019059 でコンテンツを検索します。
5）検索後、ダウンロード用ボタンをクリックし、以下のパスワードを入力します。個別ダウンロードページから、コンテンツをダウンロードしてください。

　　パスワード　→　shibata059

※サービスの内容は、予告なく変更する場合がございます。あらかじめご了承ください。

Story 1
🎧 002-010

HAPPY BIRTHDAY
by
Barry Yourgrau

ハッピー・バースデイ
バリー・ユアグロー

　バリー・ユアグローの超短篇小説は、ほとんど全部現在形で書かれている。一般論として、現在形の語りは、過去形を使った語りに較べて、先行きが見えない感覚が強まる。過去形の語りは、すべてを終わったこと、完結したこととして見る地点から語っているように響くので、安定感のようなものが伴うのに対し、現在形の語りにはそれがない。
　そのせいか、何十年か前から、未来の見通しがますます不透明になってきた世相を反映するかのように、アメリカの小説は(特に短篇は)現在形で語られることが多くなっている。
　でも、バリー・ユアグローの小説の現在形は、そういう、社会の不安と結びついた現在形とはちょっと違う。それは、一瞬先にはどんなことだって起きうる、条理も不条理も等しく可能な、夢の世界と直結した現在形である。あたかも語り手自身、次はどうなるのかよくわからないまま出たとこ勝負で語っているような、そういう自在さが、ユアグローの小説の奇想天外ぶりを支えている。あなただったら、一匹の猿がバースデイ・パーティを開こうと思い立つ、という出だしから、どんなふうに展開する物語を作るだろうか。可能性は無限である。

🎧002

A monkey wants a birthday party. A real one, with a cake and colored hats and ❶streamers and irritating noisemakers, like the ones the kids who visit the zoo always boast about. The other monkeys burst out laughing.

"A *birthday party?*" they ❷hoot. "Hello, pal? You're a monkey, remember?"

🎧003

But a couple ❸zookeepers take pity on the monkey. They purchase a cake, ❹out of their own funds, and ❺all the party trimmings too. Actually, they do this not out of pity, but to amuse themselves. It's an exploding cake, you see. They're the sort of zookeepers, ❻rare enough thankfully, who don't mind having fun ❼at a monkey's expense.

🎧004

The monkey's ❽big day arrives. The ❾primate cage ❿flutters with streamers. Colorful little pointed hats are distributed to all the monkeys, who wear them nervously and shyly, ⓫a little overcome with the luxury. ⓬Noisemakers toot and squawk. And then the candles of ⓭the great banana-crème frosted birthday cake are lit.

🎧005

At this point the no-good zookeepers ⓮edge away from the cage, grinning. ⓯The poor unwitting happy monkey takes a huge breath to blow out the candles for its birthday wish. ⓰It takes such an im-

---

❶ streamers: 色テープ、飾りテープ　❷ hoot: 素っ頓狂な声を上げる、あざ笑う　❸ zookeepers: 動物園の飼育係　❹ out of their own funds: 自分のポケットマネーで　❺ all the party trimmings: パーティのいろんな飾り　❻ rare enough thankfully: 幸いめったにいないけれど　❼ at a monkey's expense: 猿をダシにして　❽ big day: 待ちに待った日、(結婚式などの) 大切な日　❾ primate: 霊長類　❿ flutters with streamers: 飾りテープがはためく　⓫ a little overcome with the luxury: そんな贅沢にいささか気後れして　⓬ Noisemakers toot and squawk: 鳴り物が

一匹の猿が、バースデイ・パーティを開きたいと思いたつ。本物の、ケーキが出され、みんなが色つきのハットをかぶって、飾りテープや騒々しい鳴り物もあるパーティ。動物園にやって来る子供たちがいつも自慢しているようなパーティを、猿は開きたい。ほかの猿たちは大笑いする。
　「バ̇ー̇ス̇デ̇イ̇・パ̇ー̇テ̇ィ̇だって？」と猿たちは素っ頓狂な声を上げる。「おいおい、お前は猿なんだぜ、忘れたのか？」
　だが動物園の飼育係二人が、猿に同情してくれる。二人は自分のポケットマネーでケーキを買ってくれるし、パーティ用の飾りもあれこれ揃えてくれる。といっても、実は同情心からそうしているのではなく、自分たちで面白がるためにやっているのだ。つまり、そのケーキは、爆弾入りケーキなのである。この二人、幸いめったにいないけれど、猿を平気でダシにして、自分たちは楽しむたぐいの飼育係なのだ。
　猿にとって待ちに待った日がやって来る。霊長類の檻じゅうに飾りテープがはためく。カラフルな、小さなとんがり帽子が、猿全員に配られる。そんな贅沢にいささか気後れして、猿たちはそれを落ち着かなげに、照れくさそうにかぶる。鳴り物がプープー、キーキー鳴る。やがて、大きな、アイシングをまぶしたバナナクリームのケーキに、蠟燭がともされる。
　それとともに、性悪（しょうわる）の飼育係たちは、ニヤニヤしながらそっと忍び足で檻から離れていく。そうとは知らぬ哀れな猿は、喜色満面、誕生日の願いをこめて蠟燭を吹き消そうと、大きく大きく息を吸い込む。あんま

プープー、キーキー鳴る　⓭ the great banana-crème frosted birthday cake: アイシング（砂糖衣）をまぶしたバナナクリームのケーキ　⓮ edge away from . . .: ～からそっと離れていく　⓯ The poor unwitting happy monkey: そうとは知らず（unwitting）喜んでいる哀れな猿　⓰ It takes such an immense gleeful breath (that) . . .: あんまり喜んで（gleeful）、大きく大きく息を吸うものだから～　★It = The monkey

mense gleeful breath it ❶keels over backward out of its chair.

🎧006

So it's on the floor below, ❷out of harm's way, when the cake explodes with such ❸a ferocious roar that it ❹blasts a hole in the bars of the monkey cage.

🎧007

The monkey immediately ❺hops up and dashes out, while the other stunned primates slowly begin to ❻scream and chatter in the smoke and then leap in all directions, and the zookeepers ❼stagger around ❽in a deafened daze. Everyone ❾spattered with ❿charred yellow frosting.

🎧008

The monkey races along the roofs of the zoo buildings, until it reaches the zoo gates, where it ⓫leaps nimbly out into the top branches of ⓬a big shade tree outside. Grinning the whole time! It's a ⓭sly monkey, you see. It's known all kinds of zookeepers ⓮in its time, and it figured the cake was a trick. So it prepared itself, ⓯to take advantage, just in case. And ⓰off it races—to freedom!

🎧009

Happy birthday! Happy birthday!

Happy birthday . . .

This is a dream a poor monkey has, sitting on the dry branch of the tree in its monkey cage.

It sighs. And takes another slow bite of its dusty banana.

---

❶ keels over backward out of its chair: うしろに倒れて、椅子から落ちてしまう　❷ out of harm's way: 害の及ばないところに　❸ a ferocious roar: すさまじい轟音　❹ blasts a hole: ぽっかり穴を空ける　❺ hops up and dashes out: すかさず飛び上がって、檻の外へ飛び出す　❻ scream and chatter: 悲鳴をあげたりキイキイ声をあげたりする　❼ stagger around: のろのろよたよた動いている　❽ in a deafened daze: 耳を聾する爆発に呆然となって　★in a daze で「（ショック・負傷などで）呆然となって」の意。　❾ spattered with . . .: 〜が体中に飛び散って

り喜んで、大きく大きく息を吸うものだから、猿はうしろに倒れて、椅子から落ちてしまう。

　というわけで、ケーキがすさまじい轟音とともに爆発するとき、猿は床に落ちていて、害も及ばない。爆発の衝撃で、猿の檻の鉄格子にぽっかり穴が空く。

　猿はすかさず飛び上がって、檻の外へ飛び出す。ほかの霊長類たちは、ただもう啞然としているが、やがて煙の中、悲鳴をあげたりキイキイ声をあげたりし、てんでにそこら中を跳びはねる。飼育係二人は、耳を聾する爆発に呆然となって、のろのろよたよた動いている。みんな、黄色く焦げたアイシングが体中にこびりついている。

　誕生日の猿は、動物園の建物の屋根から屋根を飛んでいって、ついには動物園の門にたどり着き、そこからひょいと、外の大きな木のてっぺんの枝に飛び移る。猿はずっとニタニタ笑っている！　そう、この猿、実は抜け目ない猿なのだ。これまでありとあらゆるたぐいの飼育係に接してきたから、ケーキがいたずらだということもしっかり見抜いていたのである。だからちゃんと心の準備は出来ていて、スキあらばチャンスは逃すまいと構えていたのだ。こうして猿は去っていく ── 自由に向かって！

　ハッピー・バースデイ！　ハッピー・バースデイ！
　ハッピー・バースデイ……
　これは一匹の哀れな猿が見る夢だ。檻の中に植わった木の、乾いた枝に座って、猿が見る夢。
　猿はため息をつく。そして埃っぽいバナナを、のろのろともう一口齧(かじ)る。

❿ charred: 黒焦げになった、炭になった　⓫ leaps nimbly out into . . .: ひょいと〜に飛び移る　⓬ a big shade tree: 大きな緑陰樹　⓭ sly: 抜け目ない　⓮ in its time: これまでに、長い人（猿？）生で　⓯ to take advantage, just in case: あわよくば (just in case) チャンスは逃すまいと　⓰ off it races: 猿は去っていく　★副詞 off が倒置されて前に出てきている。

ハッピー・バースデイ／バリー・ユアグロー　017

🎧**010**

And that's our story. It's not a happy one; but then all bananas aren't fresh and golden, and all dreams don't come true.

And so the monkey's sad, and I'm sad, and you're sad.

これが私たちの物語だ。幸せな物語ではない。でもバナナがみんなみずみずしく黄金色とは限らないし、夢だってかなうとは限らない。
　というわけで猿は悲しいし、私も悲しいし、あなたも悲しい。

Story 2
🎧 011-060

FOLIE A DEUX
by
Rebecca Brown
私たちがやったこと
レベッカ・ブラウン

　もうこれまで三千万回くらい言われてきたことだが、日本語は人称代名詞が豊富であり、Iという英語の一人称単数に対して、私、僕、あたし、俺、自分、我輩……等々訳語の選択肢は無数にある。ただし、普通なら、そのIが男性か女性かによって、可能性もかなり絞られてくる。
　もしまだあなたがこの作品の邦訳をお読みになっていないなら、ぜひ原文を読むか聞くかして、このIが、そしてyouが、どのように聞こえるか、試してみてほしい。というのもこのIとyouは、原文では、男性なのか女性なのか、決定的な決め手がないように書かれているからである。作者のレベッカ・ブラウン自身がレズビアンなので、勢い、レズビアンの人々について書いていると思われがちだが、本人は、こと愛に関しては異性愛でも同性愛でも同じような問題が生じうるのであって、レズビアンだけについて書いているとは見てほしくないと述べている。このような書き方も、そういう意識から自然に生まれているのだろう。女／男、男／女、男／男、女／女という4つの可能性がこのI/youにはあるわけだが、これまで授業などで読んだ限り、男／男と読んだ人はまだいない。

🎧 011

❶In the interest of security, we agreed to ❷put out your eyes and burn out the insides of my ears.

This made sure we were always together. Each of us had something the other didn't have, something the other needed, and each of us knew exactly what the other needed and how to take care of the other. I read the newspaper to you and ❸the *New Yorker* and your mail and the lyric sheets to our new albums. I held your hand everywhere we walked. I told you ❹when you had on stripes and paisley. You wrote me notes about things on the radio. You described ❺cadences of the new records we bought and tapped out their melodies on my thighs when you were sitting next to me. You wrote me notes about all the things I couldn't know about anymore. You took care of my phone calls.

🎧 012

I learned to read your lips perfectly and ❻worked on my "strong silent type" image that could excuse me from taking part in conversation much. You got very good at sensing physical presences and ❼only bumped into things infrequently. You got new glass eyes and ❽tinted glasses. You ❾cultivated an "imaginative genius" image that acted as ❿your cover for your staring into space and ⓫missing out on physical details. You held my arm casually and easily so it looked like we were just young lovers, comfortable and excited and eager to be with each other constantly. We figured out Morse code

---

❶In the interest of security: 安全のために　❷put out your eyes: あなたの目をつぶす　❸the *New Yorker*: ★政治・経済から文学までをカバーする、アメリカの総合週刊誌。　❹when you had on stripes and paisley: あなたがストライプとペーズリーを一緒に着てしまっているときは　★have on ... は「～を身に付けている、着ている」。　❺cadences: 音の流れ　❻worked on my "strong silent type" image:「無口で力強いタイプ」というイメージを築いていった　★work on ... は「～に取り組む」。　❼only bumped into things infrequently: 何かにぶつかることもそれほ

安全のために、私たちはあなたの目をつぶして私の耳の中を焼くことに合意した。
　こうすれば私たちはいつも一緒にいるはずだ。二人ともそれぞれ、相手が持っていないもの、相手が必要としているものを持っているのであり、二人ともそれぞれ、相手に何が必要なのか、相手をどう世話したらいいかが完璧にわかっているのだ。私はあなたに新聞や『ニューヨーカー』を読んであげ、あなた宛ての手紙や、二人で新しく買ったアルバムの歌詞カードも読んであげた。二人でどこを歩くにも、あなたと手をつないだ。あなたがストライプとペーズリーを一緒に着てしまっているときは、そう教えてあげた。ラジオで言っていることを、あなたはメモに書いてくれた。新しいレコードの音の感じも説明してくれたし、並んで座っているときは私の太腿をとんとん叩いてメロディーを伝えてくれた。私にはもう知りようのないことを、あなたはみんなメモに書いてくれた。私の電話にも対応してくれた。
　私はあなたの唇が完璧に読めるようになり、会話にあまり加わらずに済むよう「無口で力強いタイプ」というイメージを築いていった。あなたは物があるのを感じとるのがとても上手になり、何かにぶつかることもそれほど頻繁ではなくなった。あなたはガラスの義眼と色眼鏡も揃えた。ぼんやり虚空に目を向けていたり、物の細部を見逃したりしても不審に思われぬよう、「想像力に富む天才」のイメージをあなたは育んだ。あなたは私の腕にごく自然にさりげなくつかまり、私たちはどこにでもいる恋人たちみたいに見えた。リラックスして、わくわくして、いつも一緒にいたくて仕方ない若い恋人たちみたいに。私たちは二人のあいだ

ど頻繁ではなくなった　❽tinted glasses: 色眼鏡　❾cultivated: 〜を育んだ　❿your cover for . . .: (真実など)を隠すための見せかけ　⓫miss(ing) out on . . .: 〜を逃す

between us. I read the book aloud to you; you tapped it out to me. What others would think was a nervous habit or a desire for physical contact was really the secret and necessary and only form of communication common to both of us.

🎧013

We took things slowly and carefully. We stayed home alone together for a long time until we thought we were normal enough to get by outside and normal enough so no one could tell. We didn't want anyone to know; it was our secret.

🎧014

You had told your public you were going to ❶lock yourself up with your new work for a while. The day of your return concert was the first day we had left the house. We went to the Center to practice. I told the ❷stagehands they must keep the piano and bench exactly where they were: ❸"Not a fraction of an inch off," I said. ❹"Acoustics," you said. They obliged. It was the first time we'd spoken with or seen anyone who'd known us before. We were each a little scared, but we ❺pulled it off just fine.

🎧015

We asked them to leave (you needed to be alone with the instrument), and they left. Then you practiced. You practiced getting from me, behind the curtain, to the piano. We walked through it together, first you holding my arm, then without my arm, me

---

❶lock yourself up with your new work: 新しい作品に集中するためいっさい人前に出ない　❷stagehands: 舞台係、裏方　❸"Not a fraction of an inch off,": 1ミリでも動かしちゃ駄目よ★a fraction of . . . は文字どおりには「〜分の1」。　❹"Acoustics,":「音響が変わってしまうからね」　★acoustics は「音響効果」。　❺pulled it off just fine: うまくやってのけた　★pull . . . off は「(困難なこと)を首尾よくやり遂げる」。

だけで通じるモールス信号を編み出した。私はあなたに本を読んであげた。あなたは聞いたことを、とんとんとモールスで私に伝えてくれた。はた目にはせわしない癖か、触れあっていたいという欲望に見えそうなものは、実は私たち二人に唯一共通する、秘密の、なくてはならないコミュニケーションの手段だった。

　私たちはいろんなことをゆっくり、じっくりと進めていった。二人きりでずっと家にこもって、これでもう大丈夫、ここまでノーマルになったら外でもやって行けるし誰にも気づかれないと思えるようになるまで外に出なかった。私たちは誰にも知られたくなかった。それは私たちの秘密だった。

　新しい作品に集中するためしばらくはいっさい人前に出ない、とあなたはあらかじめ公言していた。あなたの復帰コンサートの日が、私たちがはじめて家を出た日だった。私たちはセンターへ練習に行った。私は舞台係たちに、ピアノと椅子は絶対に動かさないようにと言った。「一ミリでも動かしちゃ駄目よ」と私は言った。「音響が変わってしまうからね」とあなたは言った。彼らは素直に従ってくれた。かつての私たちを知っていた人間と会ったり話したりしたのはこれがはじめてだった。二人とも少しびくびくしていたけれど、うまく行った。

　私たちは舞台係たちに外に出てくれと頼み（あなたが一人きりで楽器と向きあう必要があるからと言って）、彼らは出ていった。それからあなたは練習をはじめた。カーテンの蔭にいる私のそばから、ピアノのところまで行く練習を。まず二人一緒に最後まで歩いていく。はじめはあなたが私の腕につかまって、次はつかまらずに私はただそばを歩くだけにし、それ

walking beside you, then by yourself. After several times you could do it perfectly. You didn't touch the keys.

🎧016

That night I was with you ❶until right before you went on. I let you go, then ran to my seat in the middle box on the right, the best acoustics in the house. When I got to my seat, I read the program over again, satisfied with the name we'd chosen for the first piece. When I finished reading and looked up, you were well into the first piece. I was sorry I'd missed so much. For a second I was afraid you'd forget something or make a mistake, but I needn't have worried; you always had all your concert work memorized perfectly and you knew your way around a keyboard perfectly. I watched your beautiful shoulders ❷contract. I watched the way you snapped your head back at the end of the first piece. I saw the tiny points of gold on the bottom of your chin where the light caught your sweat. I felt the strength and stiffness of your ❸thighs and calves when you pressed the pedals. I imagined the stiffness of your jaw and ❹the way your teeth clenched when I had seen you practice at home. You were beautiful.

🎧017

When it was over you stood up to bow. It was the best I'd ever seen you do. Everyone clapped. I saw hundreds of pairs of hands clapping and people ❺rising to applaud. I stood up and ❻clapped furiously. I shouted, "Bravo! Bravo! Bravo!" I ❼was beaming with

---

❶until right before you went on: あなたが舞台に出る直前まで　❷contract: 縮こまる　❸thighs and calves: 腿とふくらはぎ　❹the way your teeth clenched: 歯を食いしばる姿　★clench は「食いしばる、きっと結ぶ」。　❺rising to applaud: 立ち上がって喝采し　❻clapped furiously: 力いっぱい拍手した　❼was beaming with pride: 誇りに目を輝かせていた

から今度はあなた一人で。何回か練習を重ねた末、あなたは完璧にできるようになった。鍵盤にぶつかったりはしなかった。

　その夜、あなたが舞台に出る直前まで私はあなたと一緒にいた。いよいよ時間になって、私はあなたから手を離し、ホールの右手まん中、一番音響のいいブロックの席に飛んでいった。席に着くと、もう一度プログラムを読み、一曲目に二人で決めた曲名にあらためて満足した。読み終えて顔を上げると、あなたはもうとっくに演奏をはじめていた。ずいぶん多くを逃してしまって私は残念だった。一瞬、あなたが何か忘れてしまうんじゃないか、間違えてしまうんじゃないかと不安になったけれど、そんな心配は無用だった。あなたはいつだって、コンサートの作品をすべて完全に覚えているのだ。鍵盤上の指の動きをあなたは完全に把握していた。あなたの美しい肩が縮こまるのを私は見守った。一曲目の終わりに首をさっとうしろにそらす姿を私は見守った。あなたのあごの先、光があなたの汗を捉えたところに、金色の小さな点がいくつか見えた。ペダルを踏むときのあなたの腿とふくらはぎの力強さと固さを私は感じた。あなたのあごの固さを私は思い描き、あなたが家で練習しているときに歯を食いしばる姿を思い描いた。あなたは美しかった。

　終わると、あなたは立ち上がってお辞儀をした。いままで見たなかで一番華麗なパフォーマンスだった。みんなが拍手した。何百対もの手が叩かれ、人々が立ち上がって喝采するのが見えた。私も立ち上がり、力いっぱい拍手した。私は叫んだ。「ブラボー！　ブラボー！　ブラボー！」。誇りに目を輝かせ、なおも「ブラボー！　ブラボー！」と叫ん

pride and I kept shouting, "Bravo! Bravo!" You must have heard my voice because I saw you look for me. You turned your head toward every part of the auditorium trying to hear exactly where my voice was coming from. You looked like you were ❶lost. I stopped shouting and ❷ran down to get you. As I ran I noticed people ❸glancing at me, then glancing away. I figured they probably knew I was yours, the one to whom the concert had been dedicated, ❹as noted in the program. I went backstage to where I'd left you before the concert. You ❺had just walked offstage. I grabbed you and held you. I felt the heat and moisture of your sweat through your clothes. Your muscles felt tight as they always did after a concert, but you ❻sank into me as if you didn't have bones. Within minutes, friends and people from the Center came up to congratulate you. They patted you on the back and shook your hand. They did the same to me, smiling and talking. But there was too much at once and I couldn't see what anyone was saying; I wasn't used to reading anybody's lips but yours. You nodded and smiled graciously. You held onto my arm and ❼thanked the voices. I nodded slightly and smiled. People shook my hand. Then I felt your fingers on my palm and I read, "Let's leave." You leaned close to me. I ❽smelled your flesh and felt the heat of your face against mine. I put my arm around you and we left. I walked straight to ❾where

---

❶lost: 途方にくれている　❷ran down to get you: あなたの元へ走っていった　★get は「(人)を迎えに行く」。*e.g. She's gone to get the kids from school.*（彼女は学校に子供たちを迎えに行った）　❸glancing at me, then glancing away: 私をチラッと見てそれから目をそらして　❹as noted in the program: プログラムに書いてあるとおり　❺had just walked offstage: ちょうど舞台から戻ってきたところだった　★offstage は「舞台裏へ、舞台のそとに」。　❻sank into me: 私の腕のなかに倒れ込んできた　❼thanked the voices: 人々の声に向かって礼を言った　❽smelled your

だ。あなたにも私の声が聞こえたにちがいない、なぜならあなたが私を探すのが見えたから。あなたはコンサートホールのあらゆる部分に顔を向け、私の声がどこから出ているのか知ろうとしていた。あなたは途方に暮れているように見えた。私は叫ぶのをやめて、あなたの元へ走っていった。走りながら、人々が私をチラッと見てそれから目をそらしていることに気がついた。たぶんみんな、私があなたのものだということを、プログラムに書いてあるとおりこのコンサートが捧げられた当人だということを知っているのだろう。私は舞台裏の、コンサート前にあなたを残していった場所に行った。あなたはちょうど舞台から戻ってきたところだった。私はあなたに飛びつき、抱きしめた。服を通して、あなたの汗の熱と湿り気が伝わってきた。コンサートのあとはいつもそうだけど、あなたの筋肉は固く感じられ、にもかかわらずあなたはまるで骨がないみたいに私の腕のなかに倒れ込んできた。まもなく、友人たちやセンターの人たちがお祝いを言いにやって来た。彼らはあなたの背中をぽんぽん叩いて、あなたと握手した。彼らは私にも同じことをし、にこにこ笑いながら喋っていた。でもあまりにもいろんなことがいっぺんに起きていて、誰の言っていることも私には読みとれなかった。あなた以外の人の唇を読むことに私は慣れていなかったのだ。あなたは優雅にうなずき、微笑んでいた。私の腕につかまって、人々の声に向かって礼を言った。私は軽くうなずき、微笑んだ。人々は私と握手した。と、あなたの指が私の手のひらに触れた。「帰ろう」。あなたは私の方に身を乗り出してきた。私はあなたの体の匂いを感じ、私の顔に当たるあなたの顔の熱を感じた。私はあなたの体に片腕を回し、私たちはその場を去った。あなたのためにリムジンが待たせてある場所へ私はまっすぐ歩いて

flesh: あなたの体の匂いを感じた　❾ where they had a limo waiting for you: あなたのためにリムジンが待たせてある場所

they had a limo waiting for you. You kept turning behind to say, "Thank you." As we got in the limo you told the driver to take us home, ❶we weren't feeling up to the reception. I loved being with you and I loved your not wanting to be with all those other people who wanted to see you; I loved your needing me after you got off-stage.

🎧018

The driver closed the door behind us. The leather smelled like ❷Windex. ❸My hand felt squeaky against it. The ❹limo ❺pulled away. We could barely feel the movement. Everything was big and black and smooth and shiny. We held each other. Then you sat up and put your hands on my face.

🎧019

"It was beautiful," I said.

You asked me something, but it was too dark to see your lips. Your fingers tapped my palm. "How do you know?"

"You were," I answered out loud. "You were beautiful." I ❻leaned over to hold you but you pushed me back. I put my hand on your lips. I could see your face directed towards mine in the flashing lights from outside as we drove through the city. Your face was lit by blue, then white, then red, then yellow, the colors of neon signs over bars and store windows and movie ❼marquees and stoplights. You didn't say anything for several minutes. I felt the moisture of your lips where my fingers were on your mouth.

---

❶we weren't feeling up to the reception: パーティーに出る元気がなくてね　❷Windex:（商標）ウインデックス（米国Drackett社製の窓ガラス洗浄液）　❸My hand felt squeaky against it: 触れるときゅっきゅっと引っかかった　★squeakyは「キーキーいう」。　❹limo: リムジン（運転手付きの大型セダン）　★=limousine　❺pulled away: 走り出した　❻leaned over to hold you: あなたを抱きしめようと身を乗り出した　❼marquees:（劇場・ホテルなどの）入り口のひさし

いった。あなたは何度もうしろをふり返りながら「ありがとう」と言った。二人でリムジンに乗り込むと、あなたは運転手に、家に行ってくれ、二人ともパーティーに出る元気がなくてねと言った。私はあなたと一緒にいることが嬉しく、あなたに会いたがっている人たちとあなたが一緒にいたがらないことが嬉しかった。舞台から戻ってきたあとにあなたが私を必要としていることが嬉しかった。

　私たちが乗り込むと、運転手がドアを閉めてくれた。革のシートはガラス用洗剤のような匂いがした。触れるときゅっきゅっと引っかかった。リムジンは走り出した。動いていることもほとんど感じられなかった。何もかもが大きくて黒くて滑らかでぴかぴかだった。私たちは抱きあった。と、あなたが身を起こして、私の顔に両手を当てた。

　「素晴らしかったわ」と私は言った。

　あなたが何か訊ねたが、暗くて私にはあなたの唇が読めなかった。あなたの指が私の手のひらを打った。「どうしてわかる？」

　「だって素晴らしかったもの」と私は声に出して答えた。「あなた、素晴らしかった」。私はあなたを抱きしめようと身を乗り出したが、あなたは私を押し戻した。私はあなたの唇に片手を触れた。車が街を走るなか、ぴかぴか点滅する光が外から入ってきて、あなたの顔が私の方を向いているのが見えた。あなたの顔が青く照らされ、それから白く、それから赤く、それから黄色く、酒場のネオンサインや店のウィンドウや映画館のひさしや停止信号に照らされた。しばらくのあいだあなたは何も言わなかった。私は指であなたの口に触れているところに、あなたの唇の湿り気を感じた。

🎧 020

"What?" I asked.

You pulled my other hand toward you and pressed the palm against your eye. I felt the hard solid marble underneath your skin. You leaned against me. I read your fingers. "You yelled 'Bravo'?"

"Of course it was me." I looked at your face changing colors. "You mean you didn't know?"

"Not sure," you continued, "sound different. Never heard you shout."

🎧 021

You had been telling me for a while that my voice was changing. That was understandable, of course. I couldn't hear myself speak anymore, and I didn't speak much anyway. Hardly to anyone except you.

🎧 022

I wondered what I sounded like now. I had almost forgotten what I had sounded like before. But I ❶didn't want to dwell on things or miss things. Besides, I had you. And what I didn't have, you did.

🎧 023

When we got home you called the hostess of the reception and told her you were ❷too exhausted after your big return to party, but thanked her graciously. It was going to be just a short conversation, but you stayed on the phone a long time, unconsciously unbutton-

---

❶ didn't want to dwell on things or miss things: いろんなことをくよくよ考えたり、なくなったものを恋しがったりしたくなかった　★dwell on . . .は「〜を長々と考える」。　❷ too exhausted after your big return to party: 大事な復帰コンサートを終えてくたくただからパーティーには出られない　★partyは「パーティーへ出かける」。

「なあに?」と私は訊いた。

あなたは私のもう一方の手を引き寄せ、その手のひらを自分の目に押しあてた。あなたの皮膚の下にあるがっちりと硬いガラス玉を私は感じた。あなたは私に寄りかかってきた。私はあなたの指を読んだ。「君、『ブラボー』って叫んだか?」

「もちろん私よ」。色がつぎつぎに変わっていくあなたの顔を私は見た。「じゃあ、わからなかったの?」

「はっきりとはね」とあなたはつづけた。「いつもと違ったし。君の叫び声は聞いたことがないから」

しばらく前から、私の声が変わってきているとあなたは言っていた。それはそうだろう。私にはもう自分の声が聞こえないのだし、もともと私はあまり喋る方ではない。あなたと以外はほとんど誰とも喋らないのだ。

いまの私はどんな声をしているのだろう。かつて自分がどんな声だったかも、私はほとんど忘れてしまっていた。でも私は、いろんなことをくよくよ考えたり、なくなったものを恋しがったりしたくはなかった。だいいち、私にはあなたがいた。私が持っていないものは、あなたが持っていてくれるのだ。

家に帰ると、あなたはパーティーを主催してくれた女性に電話をかけて、大事な復帰コンサートを終えてくたくただからパーティーには出られないけれどお心づかいには感謝する、と丁重に礼を言った。それはごく短い会話で済むはずだったが、あなたは長いあいだ電話をつづけ、話

ing your shirt as you talked.

🎧024

I watched your face as you undressed. I tried to read your lips but it was hard because the phone was over your mouth. But I saw your face light up. During the first part of the conversation you didn't say much. You just listened and smiled and said, "Oh, thanks, thanks," nodding. You always nodded your head slightly when you said this, and put your lips together. "Oh thanks, really." In the latter part of the conversation you started asking questions. You were sitting on the side of the bed and your right hand motioned in those little forward circles, the way you always did when you asked anything. You asked short questions then ❶long ones prefaced by statements. You nodded slightly, unconsciously, to the answers. Your whole face looked like pleasure and I thought that, now, your being unable to see other people's faces, somehow made you forget anyone could see yours. Your face hid nothing anymore. Your flesh colored and shone. Your eyes were like cloudy steel balls.

🎧025

When you got off the phone you stood up and faced me. You were beaming.

"What was that all about?" I smiled to see you so happy.

"It was good. It was really, really good." Your right hand was straight, the fingers together, chopping slightly in the air towards me on "good" and "really."

---

❶ long ones prefaced by statements: 前置きのついた長い質問

しながら無意識にシャツのボタンを外していた。

　服を脱いでいくあなたの顔を私は見守った。あなたの唇を読もうとしたが、受話器が口にかかって読みづらかった。でもあなたの顔がパッと明るくなるのは見えた。はじめのうち、あなたはあまり喋らなかった。ただ相手の話を聴いて、微笑んで、「うん、ありがとう、ありがとう」とうなずく程度だった。そう言う合間にもいつも首をほんのわずかたてに振り、上下の唇を合わせるのだ。「うん、本当にありがとう」。会話の後半になると、あなたは質問をするようになった。ベッドのはじに腰かけて、前方に小さくらせんを描くように右手を動かしながら。何か人に訊ねるとき、あなたはいつもそうするのだ。はじめは質問も短かったが、そのうちに、前置きのついた長い質問になっていった。答えを聞きながら、あなたはかすかに、無意識にうなずいていた。顔全体に嬉しさがあふれていた。私は思った —— あなたは他人の顔が見えないものだから、他人にはあなたの顔が見えるということをきっと忘れてしまったのだ。もはやあなたの顔は何も隠していなかった。肌が色づき、きらめいた。あなたの目は曇った鋼(はがね)の玉のようだった。

　電話が済むと、あなたは立ち上がって私の方を向いた。顔が輝いていた。

　「何の話だったの？」あなたがすごく喜んでいるのを見て私も微笑んだ。

　「よかった。ほんとに、ほんとによかった」。あなたの右手がまっすぐのびて、指がぴったりくっつき、「よかった」と「ほんとに」に合わせて、私の方に向かってわずかに空を切った。

"The conversation?"

Your head shook. "No, the concert. She said it was really good."

"Sure it was. I told you it was. It was beautiful."

"Yeah, yeah . . ." you said quickly. You lifted your head as if you were looking at something. You didn't know how I was looking at you.

🎧026

"Didn't I tell you it was beautiful? You heard me clapping and yelling."

"Of course, baby," you said, more to ❶pacify than to agree with me. You put your hand toward me. I took it and guided it to my stomach. I was lying down, you were ❷leaning up on your side facing me. "Of course, baby, you loved it."

I reached up to your cheek.

"Not the acoustics, not the piano. She said it was me—my work."

🎧027

I wondered what you were looking at. Your skin shone with warmth. My hand slid down your cheek, cupping your chin, then down your neck.

You leaned over me to flip off the light by the bed, but I grabbed your hand and put it on my ribs, pulling you down against me.

"I have to see you," I said.

---

❶pacify: 〜をなだめる　❷leaning up on your side: 肘をついて体を横にし

「話が？」
　あなたは首を横に振った。「ううん、コンサートがだよ。ほんとによかったってさ」
「もちろんよかったわよ。そう言ったじゃない。素晴らしかったって」
「うん、うん……」とあなたは早口に言った。そして何かを見ているみたいに首を上げた。私があなたをどんなふうに見ているか、あなたはわかっていなかった。
「素晴らしかったって、私言ったでしょう？　私が拍手して叫ぶのをあなた聞いたじゃない」
「もちろんさ、ベイビー」とあなたは、同意するというより私をなだめるような口調で言った。あなたは片手を私の方に差し出した。私はその手をとって、自分のお腹に持っていった。私は仰向けに横たわっていて、あなたは肱をついて体を横にし、私の方を向いていた。「もちろんさ、ベイビー、君は気に入ってくれたよ」
　私はあなたの頬に手をのばした。
「音響でもなく、ピアノでもない。僕が —— 僕の作品がよかったって彼女は言ってくれたんだ」
　あなたは何を見ているんだろう、と私は思った。あなたの肌は暖かみを帯びて輝いていた。私の手があなたの頬を滑り降りていき、あなたのあごを包み、それから首に降りていった。
　あなたはベッドのそばの明かりを消そうと私の上に身を乗り出したが、私はその手をつかんで自分の肋骨の上に載せ、あなたを私の方に引きずり下ろした。
「あなたが見たい」と私は言った。

🎧 028

This was the first time we had done it since we'd done it.

❶Your body eased up next to me. It was warm against my skin. Your left hand moved over my ribs. You had told me how you liked ❷the leanness of my body, the way the ribs were hard and near the surface of my skin, and the spaces between them soft and ❸giving. I ran my hand up your spine slowly, then onto your shoulders. You put your head on my neck. I felt the movement of your stomach and chest as you breathed. I looked up through your hair to the overhead light. Its two bulbs were hidden by a square, curved, milky-white shade. I saw the small black dots of dead bugs dropped in the shade, the plastic white button that screwed the shade to the fixture. I felt a film of moisture on ❹the small of your back.

🎧 029

That time you were quicker. I'd never noticed the way your skin changed color from your neck up. Your face got pink, then apricot. Your lips read out my name over and over. You put your lips together then dropped them, blowing out. Your tongue fell behind your bottom teeth. Then you ❺inhaled with your mouth and I watched you say my name again and again, faster, until you didn't say it anymore. Your eyelids shook. Then you sank like a rag. Your mouth was open. Your whole body was pink. I looked up at the ceiling. The light was still on. You hadn't seen anything and nothing had happened to me.

---

❶Your body eased up next to me: あなたの体から力が抜けて、私の体に寄りそった　★ease upは「やわらぐ、ゆるむ」。　❷the leanness of my body: 私の体の痩せた感じ　❸giving: 押すとたわむ　★giveは「（圧力などを受けて）動く、たわむ」。　❹the small of your back: あなたの腰のくびれ　❺inhaled with your mouth: 口を開けて息を吸い込んだ

FOLIE A DEUX by Rebecca Brown

あのことをして以来、私たちがするのはこれがはじめてだった。
　あなたの体から力が抜けて、私の体に寄りそった。私の肌に触れるあなたの体は暖かだった。あなたの左手が私の肋骨の上を滑っていった。私の体の痩せた感じが好きだと前にあなたは言った。肋骨が固くて肌の表面近くまで来ている感じとか、骨と骨のあいだの空間が柔らかくて押すとたわむ感じとかが。私は片手をあなたの背骨に沿ってゆっくりのぼらせていき、やがて肩に載せた。あなたは私の首筋に頭を載せた。息をするあなたのお腹と胸の動きを私は感じた。顔を上げると、あなたの髪の毛を通して天井の明かりが見えた。二つの電球は、四角い、カーブのついた乳白色のシェードに隠れていた。シェードのなかに落ちた虫の死骸の小さな黒い点がいくつか見えた。シェードを本体に留めている白いプラスチックのボタン型ネジが見えた。あなたの腰のくびれに、うっすらとした水気の膜を私は感じた。
　今回はあなたの方が早かった。あなたの肌が首から上で色が変わるさまに私はいままで気づいていなかった。あなたの顔がピンクに染まり、それからアンズ色になった。あなたの唇が私の名前を何度も何度も口にした。あなたは両の唇を合わせ、ぱっとつき出して私の名前を吐き出した。あなたの舌が下の歯の裏側に落ちた。それからあなたは口を開けて息を吸い込み、あなたが私の名前を何度も何度もだんだん速く言うのを私は見つめたが、やがてあなたはもう私の名前を呼ばなくなった。あなたの瞼が揺れた。それから、あなたはぼろきれのようにくずおれた。あなたの口は開いていた。体じゅうがピンクに染まっていた。私は天井を見上げた。明かりはついたままだった。はじめからずっと、あなたは何も見ていなかったし、私には何も起きていなかった。

🎧**030**

Our second excursion out, we went to the ❶travelling exhibit of Turner's work. We walked close, our arms around each other's backs. I read the guide notes and described the paintings. Your fingers asked questions on my arm or hand.

We stopped in front of the first painting.

"You know, his later stuff is so different. You can see where he comes from, like that sky, but . . ."

You squeezed my arm. Your fingers tapped, "What?"

This was the first time I'd had to describe something new to you, something important. Everything else was around our house, where you remembered.

"Well, the light is nice, the canvas is ❷sort of cluttered . . ."

You pinched me, then tapped my hand, "Picture?"

"Oh, boats, ships, I mean, and people . . ." I ❸stuttered.

You squeezed my hand. I hadn't spoken loudly enough. This had been a problem with me lately. I said again, "Ships and people."

You pulled my hand. "Title."

I leaned forward to read the card at the side of the painting. I turned you to face the painting as if you could see it. I whispered, "It's called 'The Battle of Trafalgar as seen from the Mizen Starboard Shroud of the Victory, 1806-1808'."

🎧**031**

I paused. I didn't know what to say. "Well, it's got lots of ships, a

---

❶ travelling exhibit: 巡回展　❷ sort of cluttered: やや乱雑な　❸ stuttered: 口ごもった

一緒に出かけた二度目の外出先は、ターナーの巡回展だった。私たちは寄りそって、腕をたがいの背中に回して歩いた。私は説明書きを読み、絵について説明した。あなたの指が私の腕や手に質問をした。
　私たちは一枚目の絵の前で立ちどまった。
「ねえ、ターナーの後期の作品ってずいぶん違うのよね。あの空とかは、もっと前の作品の面影もあるけど、でも……」
　あなたは私の腕をぎゅっと握った。指がとん、と動いた。「何？」
　あなたに何か新しいもの、大事なものを説明することになったのはこれがはじめてだった。いままではみんな家のなかのものばかりだったから、あなたにも記憶があったのだ。
「うん、だから、光が素敵だし、カンバス全体がこう、乱雑な感じで……」
　あなたは私の体をつねり、それから私の手をとんとん叩いた。「絵？」
「あ、うん、ボートでしょ、船でしょ、それに人……」私は口ごもった。
　あなたは私の手をぎゅっと握った。私の声の大きさが十分でなかったのだ。最近の私はこれが問題だった。私はもう一度、「船と人」と言った。
　あなたは私の手を引っぱった。「タイトル」
　私は身を乗り出して、絵のかたわらのカードを読んだ。あたかもあなたの目が見えるかのように、私はあなたの体を絵の方に向けた。私はひそひそ声で言った。「題はね、『トラファルガー海戦、旗艦ヴィクトリー号後檣 右舷ロープから見た光景　1806-08』」
　私は言葉を切った。何と言ったらいいかわからなかった。「ええとね、

dozen or so, and a dock going out. Some people on the dock, a priest kneeling down, not really kneeling though, and six or eight soldiers, red uniforms with white stripes across their chests, a guy with a George Washington hat, and a bunch of yellow steam, gold really, morning light, and ❶stays hanging down."

🎧 032

I stopped talking and just looked at it, then stepped back, pulling you with me, to see how it looked from three feet away.

"I didn't even notice that from up close."

You tugged my arm quickly, then released it, "What?"

I whispered, "Some of those stays go exactly like this." I dropped your hand to make a pyramid shape with my arms, but you snatched my arm back before I could gesture. I was surprised because always before, whenever you were afraid and needed to grab me, I would know it first. You would ❷gasp a little and I would hold you before your fear had a chance to set in.

🎧 033

"What?"

You grabbed my palm and tapped frantically while you whispered in my ear. But I ❸was so distracted by your mouth next to my ear that I couldn't understand your fingers on my hand. I clasped your hand and moved my head away from yours.

---

❶ stays hanging down: 船のロープがマストから垂れて　★stayは「マストの先から張ってある索」。
❷ gasp a little: はっと軽く息を呑む　❸ was so distracted by: 〜で気が散って

船がたくさん、一ダースくらいかな、あって、桟橋が突き出てる。桟橋に人が何人かいて、司祭さまが一人ひざまずいていて、と言ってもほんとにひざまずいてるんじゃないんだけど、それと六、七人兵隊がいて、赤い軍服で白い縞が胸にあってね、あと一人、ジョージ・ワシントン帽をかぶってる男がいるわ、それで黄色い蒸気、っていうかほとんど金色なんだけど、とにかく蒸気がかたまっていて、朝の光があって、船のロープがマストから垂れてるの」

　私は喋るのをやめて、ただ絵を眺め、それから、一メートル離れたらどう見えるかと、あなたも一緒に引っぱってうしろに下がってみた。

「近くからだと気づきもしなかったわ」

　あなたは私の腕をせわしなく引っぱり、離した。「何？」

　私はささやいた。「ロープがね、ちょうどこんな感じなの」。私はあなたの手を下ろして自分の両腕と一緒にピラミッドを作ろうとしたが、私がジェスチャーをする間もなくあなたは私の腕をさっとつかみ直した。私はびっくりした。なぜなら、これまではいつも、あなたが何かを怖がっていて私にしがみつく必要があるときは、かならず私の方が先にそれをわかったのだ。あなたがはっと軽く息を呑む、すると私は恐怖があなたの心に入り込んでくる前にあなたを抱きしめたのだ。

「何？」

　あなたは私の手のひらを乱暴につかみ、狂ったようにとんとんモールスを送りながら、私の耳元に何かささやきつづけた。私は耳にぴったりくっついたあなたの口で気が散って、私の手を叩くあなたの指の言っていることがわからなかった。私はあなたの手を握りしめ、自分の頭をあなたの頭から離した。

"❶Don't let go of me." Your teeth and lips were tight. I could barely read you.

"I'm sorry, I just wanted to—"

Your fingers scratched my palm: "Don't let go."

🎧034

I looked at you. Your eyes were looking somewhere behind me.

When we got to the next painting, I was thrilled. I inhaled through my teeth.

You tugged my arm again.

"Sorry. 'Hannibal Crossing the Alps.' You know."

You shook your head.

"Come on, of course you do. It's really famous. ❷You'd recognize it."

You slapped my stomach.

"OK," I sighed, "it's black and orange. The sky is going crazy and you—you just have to feel it." I couldn't imagine what you imagined this painting would look like.

🎧035

That night in bed you leaned over me to turn out the light, the way you always did before, but hadn't since that first night after the concert when I asked you to leave it on because I needed to see you clearly and not be in the dark. I said, "What are you doing? Please don't."

---

❶ Don't let go of me: 離さないでくれ　❷ You'd recognize it: 見ればわかるわ　★You'dはYou wouldで仮定法。

FOLIE A DEUX by Rebecca Brown

「離さないでくれ」。あなたの歯と唇はぎゅっと閉じていた。あなたの言っていることが私にはかろうじて読みとれた。
「ごめんなさい、私ただ──」
あなたの指が私の手のひらを引っかいた。「離さないで」
私はあなたを見た。あなたの目は、私の背後のどこかを見ていた。
二人で次の絵の前に来ると、私はぞくっとした。歯のすきまから、私は息を吸い込んだ。
あなたがまた私の腕を引っぱった。
「ごめんね。『アルプスを越えるハンニバル』。知ってるでしょう」
あなたは首を横に振った。
「そんなことないわよ、知ってるよ。すごく有名なやつよ。見ればわかるわ」
あなたは私のお腹をぴしゃりと叩いた。
「わかったわ」と私はため息をついた。「色は黒とオレンジ。空は何かもうめちゃくちゃで、それで──それでもう、これって感じるっきゃないわ」。これがどんな絵だとあなたが想像しているのか、私には想像できなかった。

その夜ベッドのなかで、あなたは明かりを消そうと私の上に身を乗り出した。以前いつもあなたはそうやっていたけれど、コンサートの夜に消さないでと私が頼んで以来、一度もそうしていなかった。あの夜、私にはあなたをはっきり見る必要があったのだ。闇のなかにいない必要があったのだ。私は言った。「何してるの？ やめてちょうだい」

🎧036

You were up on your elbow, one arm stretched over me towards the light. Your face was straight at me. You smiled as if to comfort me. Your lips moved, "It's OK, baby, it's OK." Then it was dark and your palms were on my cheeks. You were lying down, pulling me down, too. I couldn't hear or see anything. You pulled my right hand under your neck and up over your face. You put it on your mouth. I felt your lips move and the warmth and moisture of air coming out of your mouth; you were talking. You put my left hand on your stomach. I felt the smooth skin of your stomach and your stomach muscles ❶tightening under my hand. I felt the loose skin on the back of your hand and the soft line of hair that ran ❷from your chest to your crotch and the stiff curly hair of your crotch. You pressed my hand to your moving lips, talking. I touched your neck. I could tell you were speaking aloud.

🎧037

"What are you saying?" I tried to imagine what your lips looked like.

I started up, but you pulled me down and ❸rolled on top of me. You lay over me, putting your mouth by my ear. Your lips were moving near my ear and your tongue and breath, but I couldn't hear anything. I imagined the sound of your voice saying my name out loud over and over and the sound the air made as you pulled it down into your throat with your mouth open ❹when you came,

---

❶ tighten(ing): きゅっと縮こまる　❷ from your chest to your crotch: 胸から股間にかけて
❸ rolled on top of . . . : 〜の上にのしかかってきた　❹ when you came: 絶頂に達するとともに

あなたは肱をついて、私を越えて片腕を明かりのところまでのばしていた。顔はまっすぐ私の方を向いていた。私を安心させようとするかのようにあなたは笑顔を浮かべた。あなたの唇が動いた。「大丈夫だよ、ベイビー、大丈夫」。そして部屋が暗くなり、あなたの両方の手のひらが私の頬に触れた。あなたは横になって、私を一緒に引き下ろした。私には何も聞こえず、何も見えなかった。あなたは私の右手を自分の首の下に持っていき、それから顔に持っていった。あなたはその手を口に当てた。私はあなたの唇が動くのを感じ、あなたの口から出てくる空気の暖かさと湿り気を感じた。あなたは何か喋っていた。あなたは私の左手を自分のお腹に当てた。私はあなたのお腹の滑らかな肌を感じ、私の手の下でお腹の筋肉がきゅっと縮こまるのを感じた。あなたの手の甲のゆるんだ皮膚を私は感じ、あなたの胸から股間にかけて流れる柔らかな毛と、股間の硬いカールした毛とを感じた。あなたは私の手を、動いている、喋っている自分の唇に押しつけた。私はあなたの首に触れた。あなたが声を出して喋っているのがわかった。

　「何て言ってるの？」。あなたの唇がどんなふうに見えるのか、私は想像しようとした。

　私はぱっと起き上がったが、あなたは私を引き下ろし、私の上にのしかかってきた。あなたは私の上に横たわり、口を私の耳元に持ってきた。あなたの唇が私の耳のそばで動いている、あなたの舌も息も、でも私には何も聞こえなかった。あなたの声が私の名前を何度も何度も呼ぶ音を私は想像した。絶頂に達するとともにあなたが口を開けて喉に空気を吸い込むとき空気が立てる音を私は想像した。それは私が聞いた最後

which was the same sound as the last sound I heard, the gasp you gasped as I pushed out your eyes.

🎧038

We're standing in the kitchen, ❶arm's distance apart, facing each other. I have two shiny silver teaspoons, and you, the two wood-burning pens we'd found in your old toy box at home. We raise our tools to face level. Your eyes are the color of sky. The light, cool spoons are against your cheeks. I hear ❷the soft muffled rustle of your hands against my hair, ❸the swish of your palms against my cheeks, ❹the hum of the electric burning pens. I keep my eyes open, then press the round cold spoons into your eye sockets, push the sides of them in, ❺perpendicular to your face. You try to ❻blink; I press them back. My head feels like coals. I can feel everything. I ❼clench my eyes closed. Everything is hot again. You ❽gasp.

🎧039

You gasped. I ❾jolted up, screaming. I felt the movement in my throat and vibrations in my head and I couldn't hear anything. You fell away from me but reached back to put your arms around me, your hand over my mouth. You sat up and held me.

I ❿fumbled for the light and switched it on. When I looked at you, your eyes were wide open. Your lips were saying, "It's OK, it's

---

❶arm's distance apart: 腕一本のばした距離を置いて　❷the soft muffled rustle: 柔らかにこもったさらさらという音　❸the swish: さっとこする音　❹the hum: ぶーんといううなり　❺perpendicular to ...: 〜と直角をなす　★verticalに比べて「正確に垂直であること」を表す。　❻blink: まばたきする　❼clench my eyes closed: ぎゅっと目を閉じる　❽gasp: あえぎ声を上げる　❾jolt(ed) up: がくんと身を起こす　❿fumble(d) for ...: 手さぐりで〜を探す

の音と同じ音だ。私があなたの目を押しつぶしたときにあなたが立てたあえぎと同じあえぎだ。

　私たちはキッチンで、腕をのばせば届く距離を置いて向きあって立っている。私はぴかぴか光る銀色のスプーンを二本持っていて、あなたは実家にあった古いおもちゃ箱から二人で見つけた木を焼く鏝(こて)を二本持っている。私たちはそれぞれの道具を顔の高さに持ち上げる。あなたの目は空の色だ。軽い、冷たいスプーンがあなたの頬に当たっている。あなたの手が私の髪をなでる、柔らかにこもったさらさらという音が聞こえる。あなたの両の手のひらが私の頬をさっとこする音が聞こえる、電気の通った木焼き鏝のぶーんといううなりが聞こえる。私は自分の目を開けたまま、丸い冷たいスプーンをあなたの眼窩(がんか)に押しつけ、あなたの顔にまっすぐ直角に押し込む。あなたはまばたきしようとする。私はもう一度スプーンを押し込む。私の頭が石炭のように感じられる。私は何もかもすべてを感じることができる。私はぎゅっと目を閉じる。何もかもがふたたび熱くなる。あなたはあえぎ声を上げる。

　あなたはあえぎ声を上げた。私はがくんと身を起こし、悲鳴を上げた。私は喉に動きを感じ、頭に振動を感じた。何も聞こえなかった。あなたは私から離れてうしろに倒れ込みかけたが、手をのばして両腕を私の体に巻きつけ、片手で私の口をふさいだ。そして体を起こして私を抱きしめた。
　私は手さぐりで明かりを探し、スイッチをつけた。あなたを見ると、目が大きく開いていた。あなたの唇が言っていた、「大丈夫、大丈夫、大

OK, it's OK."

We kept the light on the rest of the night and every night after that.

🎧 040

You learned ❶Braille and I learned ❷ASL. But we still didn't want anyone to know. I borrowed Braille books from the library and made it obvious to everyone I could see. One day, on a bus on the way home from the library, we sat across from a boy with a hearing aid. I watched him as ❸unobtrusively as I could. We sat next to each other, your hand on my arm, and I didn't tell you. I watched his face to see if I could tell how much he could hear. He was travelling by himself. I sent off to the American Sign Language Association for information about teaching the deaf to speak. We had agreed to tell no one, but I knew you were becoming increasingly annoyed at my inability to control my voice. And I wanted to do something about it on my own. Besides, there was no way you could find out; I was in charge of the mail.

🎧 041

But when I got the information I realized I was more interested in the articles about operations and treatments that cured some kinds of deafness. I read that in some cases there was ❹scar tissue that could be removed. I tried to figure out a way of going to see an ear specialist and leaving you alone. I thought about it for weeks.

---

❶Braille: 点字（法）　★点字法を発明したフランス人Louis Braille（1809-52）の名から。　❷ASL: 手話　★American Sign Language。　❸unobtrusively: 目立たないようにして、そっと　❹scar tissue: 瘢痕組織

丈夫」と。

　私たちはその晩ずっと明かりをつけたままにしておき、その後も毎晩そうした。

　あなたは点字を学び、私は手話を学んだ。けれどそれでもまだ、私たちは誰にも知られたくなかった。私は図書館で点字の本を何冊も借り、自分の目が見えることは誰が見てもわかるようにふるまった。ある日、図書館からの帰り道に二人でバスに乗ると、補聴器をつけた男の子が向かいの席に座った。私はできるだけ目立たないようにしてその子のことを観察した。あなたは私と並んで座っていて、片手を私の腕に載せていた。けれど私はあなたには言わなかった。どれくらい聞こえるのか顔でわかるものだろうかと、私はその子の顔を観察した。その子は一人でバスに乗っていた。私はアメリカ手話協会に手紙を書いて、耳の聞こえない人たちに話し方を教える方法に関するパンフレットを送ってほしいと頼んだ。誰にも言わないということで私たちは合意していたが、私が自分の声をうまくコントロールできないことにあなたがだんだん苛立ってきているのが私にはわかっていた。だからそれについて一人で何かしたかったのだ。それに、あなたには知りようがない。郵便は私の担当なのだ。

　けれども、パンフレットが届くと、私が興味を惹かれたのはむしろ、聾（ろう）を治す手術や治療に関する記事だった。それによると、症例によっては、瘢痕組織を取り除くことができるという話だった。私はあなたを家に残して耳の専門家に診てもらいにいく手段を考えようとした。何週間もそのことを考えた。

🎧 **042**

You wrote me a note saying that the change in my voice was drastic. You wrote that it was not just a matter of tone or pitch anymore, it was my ability to form words, that sometimes I yelled and sometimes you could barely hear me, that I didn't speak clearly and I needed to work on my ❶enunciation. You wrote that maybe I'd better ❷cool it on talking until I could talk better.

Your note was ❸sloppily written. The characters bumped into each other, the lines were ❹crooked. Some of the words weren't even written completely on the page.

🎧 **043**

Our first big social occasion was the costume party. We even skipped the reception after my show at the Meyer Gallery. We went because we thought it would be safe because, if anything went wrong, we could ❺plead drunk or "in character." And, of course, we could always play up the "❻reclusive artist ill-at-ease in social situations" role. We went as two medieval saints: hair shirts, ❼stigmati, crowns of thorns, ❽the works. Any ❾social shortcomings caused by our handicaps could be excused as part of our costumes.

🎧 **044**

It was a huge party and everyone was there. I recognized some people by height and build, or if their costume was simple; you recognized their voice. But everyone was wearing masks and I couldn't

---

❶ enunciation: 発声、はっきり発音すること　❷ cool it on . . .: 〜を控える　❸ sloppily: ぞんざいに　❹ crooked: 曲がった、歪んだ　❺ plead: 〜を口実にする　❻ reclusive: 隠遁した、引きこもりがちの　❼ stigmati: 傷痕★stigmataとするのが普通。　❽ the works: 何もかも、全部　★数例を列挙した最後に付す。　❾ social shortcomings: 社交ルール上の逸脱

私の声の変化が著しくなってきたというメモをあなたは書いてよこした。もはや単に声音や高低の問題ではなく、言葉をかたちづくる能力自体の問題だ、と。喋るというよりわめくという感じのときもあればほとんど聞こえないときもあるし、話し方が不明瞭だからはっきり発音するよう練習する必要があるとあなたは書いていた。もっとうまく喋れるようになるまで、少し喋るのは控えた方がいいんじゃないかとあなたは書いていた。
　あなたのメモはぞんざいな書き方だった。字と字が重なりあい、行は曲がりくねっていた。いくつかの言葉は、なかば紙の外にはみ出してしまっていた。

　私たちがはじめて出かけた大きな社交的集いは仮装パーティーだった。マイアー・ギャラリーで開いた私の個展のあとのパーティーにさえ私たちは出なかった。なのに仮装パーティーに行ったのは、これなら安全だと思ったからだ。もし何かまずいことになったら、酔っていたからとか、「役柄を演じていたのだ」とか言い訳ができる。それに何と言っても、「社交の場では落ち着かない世捨て人タイプの芸術家」のイメージをとことん押し出せばいい。私たちは中世の聖人二人組に扮して出かけていった。ごわごわの毛衣、傷痕、茨の冠、みんな揃えて。私たちのハンディキャップが引き起こす社交ルール上の逸脱はすべて、仮装の一環ということで許されるはずだ。
　盛大なパーティーで、誰もが来ていた。背丈や体格で誰だかわかることもあれば、仮装が簡単なのでわかる場合もあった。あなたは声でわかるときもあった。でもみんな一人残らず仮面をかぶっていて、私には誰

see anyone's lips. Sometimes people came up and shook my hand or kissed me or gave me a pat on the back. I wanted to know what they were saying. I kept asking you, tapping your hand or whispering, "What are they saying? What's going on?" But you didn't want me to interrupt your conversations.

🎧045

Every time I leaned over to ask you or tap out something, I saw people ❶chuckle and nudge each other. A ❷courtier pinched me on the arm and winked, then mimicked our constant closeness by putting both arms around the ❸troubadour nearby and whispering. Later, I gave up talking with any of the faces I couldn't see.

🎧046

You and I were sitting on a couch; you were talking to two people to our right, and had been for forty minutes. My hand was on your knee. You were gesturing wildly. I felt your body shake as you laughed. You slapped your hand down on mine, grabbed it tightly, then released it. Your hands went in the air again and you weren't touching me. I thought about how familiar and common our bodies were with one another; your slapping my hand when you laughed was as natural as slapping your own thigh, as if there was no difference between them.

🎧047

Then a skeleton ❹yanked me away from the couch and pulled me out to the dance floor. I think you must have shouted after my be-

---

❶ chuckle and nudge each other: くすくす笑って (chuckle) たがいにつっつき (nudge) あう
❷ courtier: 廷臣 ❸ troubadour: トルバドゥール、吟遊詩人 ❹ yank(ed): 〜をぐいと引っ張る

の唇も読めなかった。時おり人々が寄ってきて、私と握手したり、キスしたり背中をぽんと叩いたりした。彼らが何と言っているのか私は知りたかった。何度もあなたに訊いた。あなたの手にモールスを送り、「あの人たち何て言ってるの？　何をやってるの？」とささやいた。でもあなたはほかの人たちとの会話をさえぎられるのを嫌がった。

　私が身を乗り出してあなたに何か訊ねたりモールスを送ろうとしたりするたびに、人々がくすくす笑ってたがいにつっつきあうのが見えた。一人の廷臣が私の腕をつねってウィンクし、私たちがしじゅう寄りそっているのを真似てそばの吟遊詩人の体に両腕を回して何かひそひそささやいた。しばらくすると、私はもう、見ることのできない顔たちと話すのをあきらめた。

　あなたと私はカウチに並んで座っていた。あなたは私たちの右側にいる二人と話をしていた。もう四十分前からずっと話していた。私は片手をあなたの膝に載せていた。あなたは派手にジェスチャーをしていた。笑い声を上げるあなたの体が揺れるのを私は感じた。あなたは片手で私の手をぱちんと叩き、私の手をぎゅっとつかんで、それから離した。あなたの両手がふたたび宙を舞い、あなたはもう私に触れていなかった。私たちの体がたがいをどれだけよく知っていて、どれだけ多くを分かちあっているかに私は思いをはせた。あなたが笑うときに私の手をぱちんと叩くのは、あなた自身の太腿を叩くのと同じくらい自然なことなのだ。まるでその二つのあいだには何の違いもないかのように。

　と、骸骨が私の手をぐいとつかんで私をカウチから立たせ、ダンスフロアに引っぱり出した。私があなたから引き離されたあと、あなたは

ing pulled away from you: it felt like the slow, hard pull between two magnets, then ❶the snap of release. I positioned myself facing you. You were shaking your head ❷frantically right and left. You must have been shouting because the couple next to you put their arms around you to comfort you. I imagined them telling you to settle down, that it was OK, that of course I wasn't upset with you.

🎧048

They looked at me and back at you, trying to figure us out. I waved and smiled, indicating there was nothing really wrong, that you were just the way you were sometimes, ❸high strung.

I tried to catch the rhythm of the dance from watching everyone else move. But I didn't know if I was moving on the beat or on the half-beat. I hoped the music was loud enough so my partner wouldn't try to talk to me. I felt the rhythm on the floor. I felt my blood go faster inside my ❹temples and the moisture warming inside my clothes.

🎧049

When the dance was over I came back and sat down. You threw your arms around me and put your head under my chin and on my shoulder. You were trying to cry. I felt the warmth and wetness of the sweat and ❺saliva through my costume. I felt the trembling of your body. I lifted your face up. Your eyes were closed. Your face was red but you couldn't cry. I thought how you must have felt, trying to cry but not being able to, like trying to vomit and all you

---

❶the snap of release: ぱっと離れること　❷frantically: 激しく、必死に　❸high strung: ひどく緊張した、神経が高ぶった　❹temples: こめかみ　★通例複数形で使う。　❺saliva: 唾液

きっと叫んだのだと思う。それはまるで、二つの磁石が離れまいとするような感じだった —— ゆっくり、しかし執拗に引っぱられ、やがてぱっと離れる。私はあなたの方を向くよう自分の体を据えた。あなたは首を左右に激しく振っていた。あなたはきっと叫んでいたにちがいない、隣に座ったカップルがあなたの体に腕を回してなだめていたから。私は彼らがあなたに言っているのを想像した。落ち着いて、大丈夫だよ、もちろん彼女は君のことを怒ってなんかいないさ。
　彼らは私を見て、それからまたあなたを見て、私たちがどういう仲かを探ろうとしていた。私は手を振ってにっこり笑い、べつに何も問題はないのだ、あなたはときどきこうやって神経が高ぶるのだと伝えようとした。
　私はほかの人たちの動きを見てダンスのリズムを捉えようと努めた。でも自分が一拍ごとに動いているのか半拍ごとに動いているのか、どうにもわからなかった。音楽が騒々しくて私のパートナーが話しかけてこなければいいが、と思った。私はフロアのリズムを感じた。こめかみの内側で血の流れが速くなり、服のなかで湿気が暖かくなっていくのを感じた。
　ダンスが終わると、私はカウチに戻って座った。あなたは両腕を投げるようにして私の体に巻きつけ、頭を私のあごの下に入れ、私の肩に載せた。あなたは泣こうとしていた。私の衣裳を通して、汗と唾液の暖かさと湿り気が感じられた。あなたの体の震えが感じられた。私はあなたの顔を持ち上げた。あなたの目は閉じていた。あなたの顔は赤かったが、それでもあなたは泣けなかった。泣こうとして泣けないあなたがきっと味わっている気持ちを私は考えてみた。吐こうとしているのに、

could do was ❶the dry heaves. Your stomach was moving, short and quick. You were gasping. You were holding my hand with both of yours. You were squeezing it, "Home—home—home—"

🎧 050

We both smelled like cigarettes and sweat, but neither of us showered before we went to bed. You lay there shaking without crying. I imagined the sound of your sobbing. I wanted to say something, that I was sorry: for the dance, for the party, for everything, for what we'd done. But I didn't. I didn't open my mouth because I knew I couldn't talk clearly anymore. And that, though you would probably understand me, the sound of my voice was horrible to you. I wanted to tap out "I'm sorry" on your skin. I put my hand on your naked stomach. I started to raise and lower my fingers, but I stopped. I hated talking this way, the only way we could communicate in the same way; I hated it because it was the only way.

🎧 051

I didn't tap out the words "I'm sorry" because I didn't know what they meant. And because I didn't really mean that. But I had to take the risk that you would know what I meant. That what I meant by not using our only way of communicating, our little, secret way, was that I wanted us to have a new one. That this new

---

❶ the dry heaves: 乾いたむかつき、空嘔吐

出てくるのは乾いたむかつきだけ。あなたのお腹が動いていた。短く、速く、あなたはあえいでいた。両手で私の片手を握っていた。あなたは私の手をぎゅっと握っていた、「帰ろう ── 帰ろう ── 帰ろう ── 」。

　私たちの体には煙草と汗の匂いが染みついていたが、二人ともベッドに入る前にシャワーを浴びはしなかった。あなたはベッドに横たわって、泣かずに体を震わせていた。あなたがしゃくり上げる音を私は想像してみた。私は何か言いたかった、悲しいねと言いたかった。ダンスのこと、パーティーのこと、すべてのこと、私たちがやったこと。でも私は何も言わなかった。私は口を開けなかった、なぜならもはや自分がはっきり喋れないことがわかっていたから。それと、たぶんあなたは私が何を言っているかは理解してくれるだろうけど、私の声が立てる音があなたの耳におぞましく響くことがわかっていたから。私はあなたの肌に「悲しいね」とモールスを送りたかった。あなたのむき出しのお腹に私は片手を置いた。私は指を上げ下げしはじめたが、やめた。こんなふうに話すのは嫌だった。私たちが二人とも同じようにコミュニケートできる唯一の方法で話すのは嫌だった。それが唯一の方法だから、それ以外に方法はないから、私にはそれがたまらなく嫌だった。
　「悲しいね」という言葉を私はモールスしなかった、なぜならその言葉が何を意味するのか私にはわからなかったから。それに、私が本当に言いたいことはそれじゃなかったから。私が何を言おうとしているか、あなたがわかってくれるだろうと賭けるしかなかった。私たちの唯一のコミュニケーションの手段、私たちのひそかな秘密、それを使わないことで私が言おうとしているのは、二人のあいだに新しい手段を築きたい

way was how I could tell you I would never leave you. Ever, even for an instant out in the world. That we would stay and watch out for each other.

🎧052

That was what I meant when I flattened my palm out straight and still on your stomach and put my head on your chest to sleep.

But I don't know if you knew what I meant; you were almost still; your sobbing had stopped. I think we slept.

🎧053

So we didn't go out again. We stayed inside with one another. During the day you composed and I painted. At night we read or I watched TV and you listened to the radio in our room. It was nice because we fit each other like glove and hand. If I wanted to go to sleep early but you wanted to listen to the radio, the noise didn't bother me. I could fall asleep in your arms while you listened to the ❶*1812 Overture*. Or if you wanted to sleep and I wanted to watch TV, I could keep it on and ❷the flickering of the screen wouldn't bother you.

Our house was warm and peaceful. We shared everything. What was yours was mine; what was mine was yours. We had no ambitions and no fear.

🎧054

One night I wanted to stay up and ❸do some studies for my new

---

❶ *1812 Overture*: ★チャイコフスキー (1840-93) 作曲の演奏会用序曲。　❷ the flickering of the screen: 画面のちかちか　❸ do some studies: 試作を作る　★studyは「習作、スケッチ」。

と私が思っているということだ。この新しい手段を使って私はあなたに伝えるのだ、私はあなたから決して離れはしないと。絶対に、この世に在るかぎり一瞬たりとも。私たちはいつまでも一緒で、いつまでも守りあうのだ。

　手のひらをぴんとのばしてあなたのお腹の上に当て、頭をあなたの胸に載せて眠ろうとしたときに私が言おうとしていたのはそういうことだった。

　でも私が言おうとしていたことをあなたがわかってくれたかどうか、私にはわからない。あなたはほとんどまったく動かなかった。しゃくり上げも止んでいた。私たちは眠ったのだと思う。

　そんなわけで私たちはもう外出しなかった。家にこもって、二人きりで過ごした。昼のあいだにあなたは作曲し、私は絵を描いた。夜は一緒の部屋で読書をしたり、私がテレビを見てあなたはラジオを聴いたりした。それは素敵な暮らしだった。私たちは手袋と手みたいにしっくり合っていた。もし私が早寝したくてあなたがラジオを聴きたくても、音が私の邪魔になることもない。『一八一二年序曲』を聴いているあなたの腕に抱かれながら私は眠りに落ちることができるのだ。逆にあなたが眠りたくて私がテレビを見たくても、つけっ放しの画面のちかちかにあなたがわずらわされたりもしない。

　私たちの家は暖かく、ひそやかだった。私たちはすべてを分かちあった。あなたのものは私のもの、私のものはあなたのものだった。私たちには何の野心もなく、何の恐怖もなかった。

　ある夜、私は新作『声たち』の試作を作るために遅くまで仕事をしよ

piece, *Voices*. It was a huge red-orange fiery roundish globe with lines of blue and white curling over it. It was an abstract piece about the sound the air made when you pulled it down into your throat with your mouth open.

🎧055

I was very taken with my work then. Sometimes I would stay up working very late. My canvases had grown huge. My work was very physical and massive. I knew I must have made lots of noise, so I worked downstairs where you couldn't hear me.

🎧056

That night I worked till three. When I started upstairs to our room, something smelled wrong. As I reached the ❶landing I saw the light in our room was off. I wondered if it had burnt out because we always kept it on for me. You would never have turned it off. But when I reached the top of the stairs I saw into our room.

🎧057

You were ❷sprawled on the bed in a pool of blood. Your neck and stomach and crotch and hands and face and mouth were red. The sheets were red. I didn't know you had so much blood. And there kept on being more.

🎧058

Then I heard the sound of the running blood and I heard the sound inside myself of mine. Inside of me it sounded like snow, like I was driving into a tunnel under snow. I hadn't heard like that

---

❶ landing:（階段の）踊り場　　❷ sprawl(ed): 大の字に寝そべる

うと思った。それは炎のように赤っぽいオレンジの巨大な球の上に、青と白の線がカールしている作品だった。あなたが口を開けて喉に空気を吸い込むときに空気が立てる音についての抽象的な作品だ。

　そのころ私はこの作品に没頭していた。夜更けまで仕事をすることもあった。いまやカンバスはおそろしく大きくなっていた。私の作品はとても物質的で、量感があるのだ。作業中は相当大きな音を立てるとわかっていたから、あなたに聞こえないよう仕事は一階でやった。

　その夜、私は三時まで仕事をした。階段をのぼって私たちの部屋へ向かうと、何か変な臭いがした。踊り場まで来ると、私たちの部屋の明かりが消えているのが見えた。電球が切れてしまったのだろうか。なぜなら明かりはいつも私のためにつけておくことにしていたからだ。あなたが消してしまうはずはない。でもとにかく、階段をのぼり切ったところで私たちの部屋を覗いてみた。

　あなたはベッドの上で、血の池のなかに大の字に倒れていた。首もお腹も股間も両手も顔も口も赤かった。シーツも赤かった。あなたのなかにこんなに血があるなんて知らなかった。そして血はまだまだ出てきていた。

　と、流れる血の音が聞こえ、私のなかの、私自身の血の音が聞こえた。私のなかでそれは雪のような音を立て、まるで雪の下でトンネルに入っていくみたいな気がした。耳が聞こえたころだってそんなふうに聞こえ

before. It was the first thing I had heard since we had done it.

🎧059

 I walked to the bed and sat on the bed and sat beside your body and picked up the phone. I couldn't hear the dial tone but I dialed 911. I couldn't hear when they picked up the phone or if or when they answered, and I didn't know and I couldn't tell, if whoever it was could understand what I was trying to say. So I kept saying over again, "Hello? Hello? Something's happened—Hello? There's something wrong—Hello? There's someone ❶stabbed—I didn't hear—I couldn't hear—Hello?"

🎧060

 I stayed on the phone and repeated this over and over because I didn't know when someone would answer, or how long it would take to understand, or if somebody ever would, or why I couldn't say right what had happened, why I couldn't tell what we'd done.

---

❶ stab(bed): 〜を刺す

たことは一度もなかった。私たちがあれをして以来、何かが聞こえたのはこれがはじめてだった。

　私はベッドまで歩いていき、ベッドに腰かけ、あなたの体のかたわらに座って電話を手にとった。ダイヤルトーンは聞こえなかったけれど、緊急番号の911を私はダイヤルした。相手がいつ電話に出たかも私には聞こえなかったし、返事をしてくれたのか、いつしてくれたのかも聞こえなかったし、相手が誰であれ私の言おうとしていることを理解できているかどうかも私にはわからなかったし知りようもなかった。だから私は何度も何度も言いつづけた。「もしもし？　もしもし？　大変です —— もしもし？　大変なことが起きたんです —— もしもし？　人が刺されたんです —— 聞こえませんでした —— 私には聞こえないんです —— もしもし？」

　私は電話口にとどまって、これを何度もくり返した、なぜなら私にはわからなかったからだ、いつ誰かが電話に出てくれるのかも、理解してもらうのにどれくらいかかるのかも、そもそもいつかはわかってもらえるのかどうかも、何があったかを私がなぜうまく言えないのかも、私たちがやったことを私がなぜ言えないのかも。

Story 3
🎧 061-107

THE GREAT DIVORCE
by
Kelly Link
大いなる離婚
ケリー・リンク

　There once was a man whose wife was dead ... なんだか「昔、男ありき」みたいだが、読んでみると、単に「妻を亡くした男」などではなく、結婚生活を続けているなかで妻がずっと死者であった、というなかなか奇抜な設定である。タイトルの"The Great Divorce"にしても、実はC. S. Lewisの、天国と地獄の乖離を描いた宗教的作品のタイトルをそのまま借用し、「天国と地獄」という対立を「生者と死者」の対立にずらして使っている（まあ実はルイスの *The Great Divorce* という書名にしても、William Blakeの *The Marriage of Heaven and Hell* のもじりなのだが）。英語は易しい部類に入るだろうが、いかなる展開もありうる、ひょっとするとバリー・ユアグロー以上に奇想天外な世界を描いているので、聴くにあたっては、とにかく"Anything can happen"と自分に言い聞かせながら聴くのがいいと思う。そういう奇怪な設定のなかで、妙に切実だったり、切なかったり、あるいは単にあほらしかったり、いろんな感慨を生じさせてくれる書き手である。

🎧 061

There once was a man whose wife was dead. She was dead when he fell in love with her, and she was dead for the twelve years they lived together, during which time she ❶bore him three children, all of them dead as well, and at the time of which I am speaking, the time during which her husband began to suspect that she was ❷having an affair, she was still dead.

It has been only in the last two decades that ❸the living have been ❹in the habit of marrying the dead, and it is still not ❺common practice. Divorcing the dead is still less common. More usual is that the living husband—or wife—who regrets a marriage no longer acknowledges ❻the admittedly tenuous presence of his spouse. ❼Bigamy is easily accomplished when one's first wife is dead. It may not even be bigamy. And yet, ❽where there are children concerned, the ❾dissolution of a mixed marriage becomes ❿stickier. Thirteen years after they first met at a cocktail party in the home of ⓫a celebrated medium and matchmaker who had been both ⓬profiled in ⓭*The New Yorker* and ⓮picketed by conservative religious groups, it was clear to both Alan Robley (living) and Lavvie Tyler (deceased), that there were worse fates than death. Their marriage was ⓯as dead as a doorknob.

At least, that was what Alan Robley said.

🎧 062

Alan and Lavvie Robley-Tyler's children had communicated to

---

❶ bore A B: Aとの間にBをもうけた　★bearの過去形。　❷ having an affair: 不倫をしていて
❸ the living: 生者、生存者　★複数扱い。　❹ in the habit of . . .: 〜を習慣として　❺ common practice: 一般的な慣習　❻ the admittedly tenuous presence of his spouse: もともと希薄というほかない (admittedly tenuous) 配偶者 (spouse) の存在　❼ bigamy: 重婚　❽ where there are children concerned: 子供がいる場合は　❾ dissolution: 崩壊、解消　❿ stickier: より厄介な　★stickyは「ねばねばする」のほかに、口語で「難しい、困った」。　⓫ a celebrated medium and

昔々、妻が死んでいる男がいた。男が妻に恋したとき彼女は死んでいたし、一緒に暮らした、やはりみな死んでいる子供が三人生まれた十二年のあいだも死んでいた。これから語ろうとしている、妻が不倫をしているのではと夫が疑いはじめた時期にも、彼女はやはり死んでいた。
　生者が死者と結婚する習慣が生まれたのはつい二十年前のことにすぎないし、いまでも決して一般的ではない。死者と離婚するとなるともっと稀である。比較的普通なのは、生者である夫もしくは妻が結婚したことを後悔し、もともと希薄というほかない配偶者の存在をもはや認めなくなるというケースである。先妻が死者である場合は重婚も容易なのだ。そもそも重婚でさえないのかもしれない。とはいえ、子供がいる場合は、異種間婚の崩壊も厄介な話になりがちである。十三年前、『ニューヨーカー』でも大々的に取り上げられ、保守的な宗教団体からは抗議のピケを張られていた著名な霊媒兼結婚仲介業者の家で開かれたカクテルパーティで出会ったアラン・ロブリー（生者）とラヴィ・タイラー（死者）は、十三年を経たいま、死よりおぞましい運命があることを二人とも痛感していた。彼らの結婚はドアノブのように死んでいた。
　少なくとも、アラン・ロブリーはそう言っていた。
　ロブリー＝タイラー家の子供たちは、家庭用のプランシェットと

---

matchmaker: 著名な霊媒兼結婚仲介業者　⓬ profiled in . . .: 〜で紹介された　⓭ *The New Yorker*: ★22ページ❸参照。　⓮ picketed by . . .: 〜から抗議のピケを張られて　⓯ as dead as a doorknob: ★「完全に死んでいる」という意味の決まり文句。(as) dead as a doornailと言うことも多い。

their father, ❶via the household planchette and Ouija board, a desire to be taken to Disneyland; because divorce is always hardest on the children, and because Disneyland offered, at that time, an extraordinary discount to the dead, their medium had agreed to meet Alan Robley and his wife at Disneyland, which was only a fifteen-minute commute from her home, ❷provided Alan Robley pay her admission as well as the usual fee. Besides, the medium had always loved watching amusement park visitors wait in long, orderly lines. She found it comforting.

🎧063

The medium's name was Sarah Parminter. Her movements were economical: ❸abbreviated and curiously ungraceful. Alan Robley imagined that this was so because she could see, at all times, the dead ❹crowding around her. He himself had grown accustomed to moving slowly when he came home from work, in order to avoid unexpectedly stepping on or passing through his wife, or one of his three children. It takes great effort for the dead to make the living see them and therefore mixed marriages ❺rely on dedicated dead-spaces: areas of floor and furniture that have been ❻marked out with special red tape, red tile, squares of red fabric. (The children of the living and the dead most often ❼take after their dead parents. Life, like red hair or blue eyes, is ❽a recessive gene.)

🎧064

Alan Robley longed for a better, less complicated relationship

---

❶via the household planchette and Ouija board: 家庭用のプランシェットとウィージャ・ボードを通して　★planchetteとOuijaはともに心霊術で使われる道具。前者は心臓型をした小板で、指を軽く乗せると自動的に文字を書く。後者はplanchetteとともに用いられる、文字・数字・記号を記した占い板。日本の「こっくりさん」に近い。　❷provided (that)...: 〜という条件で、もし〜ならば　❸abbreviated and curiously ungraceful: 何もかもが縮約され、妙に優美さを欠いていて　❹crowd(ing) around...: 〜（の周り）に群がる　❺rely on dedicated dead-spaces: ★直訳

ウィージャ・ボードを通して、ディズニーランドに連れていってほしいという要望を父親に伝えてきた。離婚で一番つらい思いをするのはつねに子供たちであり、かつ、当時ディズニーランドは大幅な死者割引を提供していたので、霊媒兼結婚仲介業者の女性は、アラン・ロブリー＝タイラーが通常の料金に加えて彼女の入園料も払うことを条件に、夫婦とディズニーランドで落ち合うことに同意した。幸いディズニーランドは彼女の自宅から十五分しかかからなかったし、遊園地の入園者が整然とした長い列に並んで待っているのを見るのが彼女は好きだった。そういうのを見ていると心が安らいだ。

　霊媒は名をセアラ・パーミンターといった。彼女の動きには無駄がなかった。何もかもが縮約され、妙に優美さを欠いていた。きっと四六時中群がってくる死者が見えてしまうからだろうとアラン・ロブリーは想像していた。彼自身、仕事から帰宅すると、妻なり三人の子供の誰かなりを踏んづけたり通り抜けたりしてしまわぬよう、ゆっくりと動く癖がついていた。死者にとって、自分の姿を生者に見えるようにするのは容易ではない。だから異種間婚では、デッドスペースをきっちり確保することが鍵となる。床や家具の要所要所を、特別な赤いテープと、赤いタイルと、四角い赤い生地を用いて仕切るのだ（生者と死者の子供たちは、死んでいる方の親に似ることが多い。生とは赤毛や青い瞳と同じく劣性遺伝子なのである）。

　アラン・ロブリー＝タイラーは、子供たちとのよりよい、より厄介の

すれば「特設のデッドスペースに依存している」。生者と死者が折り合いをつけて生活していくためには「デッド」スペース（無駄な空間）が必要というギャグ。　❻ mark(ed) out with . . .：〜で仕切る　❼ take after . . .：〜に似ている　❽ a recessive gene: 劣性遺伝子　★「優性遺伝子」は a dominant gene。

with his children. He wanted to know them better. Who doesn't?

Sarah Parminter and Alan sat on an uncomfortable bench beneath a pink bougainvillea. The three Robley-Tyler children were ignoring a YOU MUST BE THIS TALL sign. There are advantages to being the child of a mixed marriage. The usual rules don't apply. Their mother, Lavvie, was sitting in ❶the crown of the bougainvillea above the bench, shaking down the papery flowers. ❷He loves me not. He loves me not. The bougainvillea hung like tiny lanterns in Alan Robley's longish hair and in the curl of his collar. He ignored them. Lavvie ❸got up to worse things. At one time, he'd found her behavior ❹endearing.

🎧065

Lavvie Tyler had stopped living sometime around the turn of the century. She'd been twenty-two and unmarried. She'd died of ❺tuberculosis. Even in death, she still trembled and coughed, silently, so that the bougainvillea shook too. She was both older and younger than her husband. Marriage and the birth of three children had only made this more true.

🎧066

"Explain this to me again, Alan," Sarah Parminter said. "You say that you and Lavvie have talked about this a great deal. You agree that there are ❻irreconcilable differences. You say you both want this. This divorce."

"Yes," Alan said. He looked away. He wore an expensive shirt, in

---

❶ the crown of . . .: 〜のてっぺん　❷ He loves me not. He loves me not: ★普通の花占いならもちろんHe loves meとHe loves me notを交互に言う。　❸ got up to worse things: もっとたちの悪い真似をやったりもした　★get up to . . .は「(いたずらなど)をしでかす」。　❹ endearing: 可愛らしい　❺ tuberculosis: 結核　❻ irreconcilable differences: (夫婦間などの)和解しがたい意見の相違

少ない関係を渇望していた。彼らをもっとよく知りたいと願った。そう思わない親がいるだろうか？

　セアラ・パーミンターとアランは、桃色のブーゲンビリアの下に置かれた座り心地の悪いベンチに座っていた。ロブリー＝タイラー家三人の子供たちは、〈これに背が届かない子は入ってはいけません〉の看板を無視していた。異種間婚の子供であることには得な面もある。通常のルールがあてはまらないのだ。母親のラヴィは、ベンチの上のブーゲンビリアのてっぺんに座って、紙のような花びらを揺すって落としていた。愛シテナイ。愛シテナイ。花びらはアラン・ロブリーの長めの髪や襟の巻き毛に落ちて、小さなちょうちんのように垂れ下がった。アランは知らん顔をした。ラヴィはもっとたちの悪い真似をやったりもする。かつてはアランも、そういう彼女のふるまいを可愛らしいと思ったものだった。

　ラヴィ・タイラーは世紀の代わり目ごろに生きるのをやめた。当時彼女は二十二歳で、未婚だった。死因は結核。死んでいるいまもなお、声もなく震え、咳込むので、それに合わせてブーゲンビリアも揺れた。彼女は夫より年上でもあり年下でもあった。結婚し、子供が三人生まれたことによって、その事実はいっそう真となった。

　「もう一度説明してくれるかしら、アラン」とセアラ・パーミンターは言った。「ラヴィと二人でこのことはじっくり話しあったのよね。どうしようもない相違があるということで意見は一致しているのね。二人ともこれを望んでいるのよね —— この離婚を」

　「その通り」とアランは言った。彼は目をそらした。アランは高価なシャツを着ている。死者が惹かれるとされている赤い色合いのシャツで

❶a shade of red that the dead were supposed to find attractive. He wore lipstick in the same shade of red, and there were greasy little ❷flecks of it on his front teeth. Red ❸fingernail polish. No doubt the soles of his shoes were red as well. Was it for Lavvie, ❹despite their difficulties, or for his children? To draw them near? Sarah wondered why the living, who were so very much more ❺solid, after all, than the dead, so often looked ❻shifty and deceitful to her. She tried not to ❼be prejudiced. But the dead were so beautiful, so fixed and so fluid, like sheets of calligraphy. They belonged to her, although she told herself that she was wrong to feel this way.

🎧067

"Lavvie says that this is your idea, not hers," Sarah said. "That's what she's telling me. She says that there have been difficulties. She admits that. She says that the children take up a great deal of her time. She says that your ❽romantic life has suffered. She says that there have been arguments. Smashed dishes, icy silences, ❾bouts of unearthly weeping. She knows that she ❿has a temper. But she says she still loves you. You don't understand her, but she still loves you. She says she wonders if you've met someone else."

🎧068

"I don't believe this!" Alan said. He laughed. He looked around, as if Lavvie might suddenly, finally, at last, ⓫materialize. But he never once looked up at the top of the bougainvillea. "Why is she saying this? I sat up all Tuesday night with the Ouija board, help-

---

❶a shade of . . . : 〜の色調　❷fleck(s): 汚れ、しみ　❸fingernail polish: マニキュア　❹despite their difficulties: なんだかんだいっても　❺solid: 実体のある　❻shifty and deceitful: ★直訳すると「ずるくて (shifty) 嘘をつく (deceitful)」。　❼be prejudiced: 偏見を抱いている　❽romantic life: ★性生活のこと。　❾bouts of unearthly weeping: この世のものとは思えないすすり泣き★bouts of . . . は「発作的に訪れる〜」。　❿has a temper: 癇癪もちである、激しやすい　⓫materialize: 実体化する

ある。唇にも同じ色合いの口紅をつけ、前歯のところどころにその脂っぽい汚れがついていた。赤いマニキュア。当然靴底も赤いはずだ。なんだかんだいってもラヴィのためだろうか、それとも子供たちのため？ 子供たちを惹きよせるためか？ 生者の方がずっと実体があるはずなのに、どうして生者はこそこそと何か隠しているように見えることが多いんだろう、とセアラは考えた。偏見を抱いてはいけないと思いつつも、死者の方がずっと美しいし、ずっと確固として、かつずっと流動的だ。カリグラフィを書いた紙みたいに。そういうふうに感じてはいけないと自分に言い聞かせるものの、死者たちは彼女のものだった。

「これはあなたが言い出したのであって彼女じゃないってラヴィは言ってるの」とセアラは言った。「私にはそういうふうに言ってるのよ。いろいろ相違があったってことは彼女も言ってる。それは彼女も認めているのよ。子供たちにすごく時間をとられると彼女は言ってる。あなたのロマンチック・ライフが衰えてしまったとも言っている。言い争いもさんざんあったと言ってる。お皿が割られて、氷のような沈黙があって、この世のものとは思えないすすり泣きがあって。自分が激しやすい性格だっていうことは彼女も自覚しているわ。それでも、まだあなたのことを愛してると彼女は言っているのよ。あなたは彼女のことを理解していないけど、それでも彼女はまだあなたを愛しているのよ。あなたに誰かほかの人ができたのかしらって彼女は言ってるわ」

「冗談じゃない！」とアランは言った。そして声を上げて笑った。彼は周りを、ラヴィがいきなり、ついに、とうとう実体化するのではないかと思っているみたいに見回した。だがブーゲンビリアのてっぺんはいっこうに見上げなかった。「なんでそんなこと言うんだ？ 僕は火曜

ing Carson and Allie and Essie with their homework, and she never said one single word to me. Carson said that Lavvie was down in the basement folding laundry, but I think it was one of the kids who was folding laundry, ❶covering up for their mother. I think Lavvie has a boyfriend. A dead boyfriend. Some days I don't even feel like the kids are mine. I love them ❷to pieces, but it's hard for me, thinking that they don't really belong to me. They already spend so much time with their mother. Who knows what she says to them about me?"

🎧069

"Lavvie says you're jealous of her friends," Sarah said. "She says she's the one who should be jealous. She says that you only married a dead woman because you like the people at your work to think you're trendy. She says she can see the way you look at living women. You're always ❸flirting with women at the grocery store. She knows you spend hours looking at porn online, and you don't even think about whether the children are there, too."

Silence. Sarah could hear Alan Robley's teeth, grinding together like pieces of chalk. Lavvie trembled in her tree.

🎧070

"Where are the kids?" Alan said. "Do me a favor, Sarah, tell the kids not to get too far away. Last time we came, Essie got lost. ❹Apparently she just kept getting on different boats at It's a Small

---

❶ cover(ing) up for . . .:（隠しごとをして）〜をかばう　❷ to pieces: めちゃくちゃに、どうしようもなく　❸ flirt(ing) with . . .: 〜といちゃつく　❹ Apparently: どうやら〜らしい

日の夜ずっと、カーソンとアリーとエシーの宿題を手伝いながら寝ずにウィージャ・ボードの前で待ってたのに、彼女は僕には一言も喋らなかったんだぞ。ママは地下室で洗濯物を畳んでるってカーソンは言ったけど、畳んでたのは子供のうちの誰かだと思うね、母親をかばっていたのさ。ラヴィにはボーイフレンドがいると僕は思うね。死んでいるボーイフレンドが。日によっては、あの子たちが自分の子に思えないこともあるんだよ。どうしようもなく愛してはいるさ、だけどつらいんだ、あの子たちが本当に僕に属してはいないんだと思えて。いまだってすでに、母親と一緒に過ごす時間の方がずっと多い。母親が僕のことを、あの子たちにいったいどう言っているやら」

「あなたが彼女の友人たちに嫉妬してるってラヴィは言ってるわ」とセアラは言った。「嫉妬してもおかしくないのは自分の方だって彼女は言ってる。あなたが死んでいる女と結婚したのは、単に職場の人たちからトレンディだと思われたいからだって彼女は言うのよ。あなたが生きている女たちを見るときの目つきはお見通しだって言っているわ。食料品店へ買い物に行くたびに女たちといちゃついてるし。インターネットでポルノサイトを何時間も見てることも彼女は知ってるのよ、あなたったら子供たちがそこにいるかどうかも考えないって」

　沈黙。アラン・ロブリー＝タイラーの歯が、チョークを嚙み合わせたみたいにぎりぎり鳴っているのがセアラには聞こえた。木の上でラヴィが震えた。

「子供たちはどこだ？」とアランが言った。「なあセアラ、頼むよ、あんまり遠くへ行くなって子供たちに言ってくれよ。こないだ来たときもエシーが迷子になったし。どうやら〈スモール・ワールド〉でいろんな

World. She was singing "It's a Small World After All" ❶in people's ears, ❷only she kept changing the lyrics. All these kids were getting off the ride ❸in tears. If Carson wants to go to Frontierland, he should come ask us. We can all walk over."

"They're still in line for Space Mountain," Sarah said. "They're beautiful kids, Alan. And even though this must be difficult for them, they're handling it so well. You and Lavvie must be very proud. Lavvie says she falls in love with you again each time she looks at them. They look so much like you, Alan."

🎧071

Alan's red lower lip was trembling now, too. Tremble, tremble: Lavvie in the bougainvillea. Tremble, tremble: Alan's lip. Sarah Parminter realized that she had begun to tap one foot in sympathy. She stopped her foot and made herself look at the faces of the people waiting in line. Dead people hung in the air, their heels resting on the shoulders of living people, and living people walked right through two dead people who were ❹making out, well, having sex ❺right there in line, ❻practically, but ❼nobody got upset. It was astonishing how well the dead and living got along under normal circumstances, just so long as they could ignore each other.

🎧072

Alan said, "I only look at other women because—because when a woman walks by, I think maybe that's how Lavvie looks. Maybe Lavvie walks fast like that. Maybe Lavvie's ass moves like that when

---

❶in people's ears: よその人たちの耳元で　❷only: (接続詞で)だが、ただし　❸in tears: 泣いて、涙を浮かべて　❹making out: いちゃいちゃして、愛撫しあって　❺right there in line: もろに列のなかで、並んだまま　❻practically: 事実上　❼nobody got upset: 誰も取り乱さなかった

ボートに乗ってたらしい。よその人たちの耳元で『イッツ・ア・スモール・ワールド』を歌ってたんだけど、歌詞をすっかり変えて歌ったのさ。ボートを降りてくる子供はみんなしくしく泣いてた。カーソンがもし〈フロンティアランド〉に行きたいんだったら、ちゃんとそう言いにこなくちゃ駄目だ。みんなで一緒に行けばいい」
　「みんなまだ〈スペース・マウンテン〉に並んでるわよ」とセアラは言った。「可愛い子供たちねえ。きっと三人ともすごくつらいでしょうけど、立派にがんばってるわよね。あなたもラヴィもさぞ鼻が高いでしょうね。子供たちを見るたびに、もう一度あなたに恋をするってラヴィは言ってるわ。みんなあなたにすごく似てるのよ、アラン」
　いまやアランの赤い下唇も震えていた。ぶるぶるぶるぶる —— ブーゲンビリアの上のラヴィ。ぶるぶるぶるぶる —— アランの唇。自分がいつの間にか同情のあまりとんとん片脚を動かしていることにセアラ・パーミンターは気づいた。足を動かすのをやめて、行列に並んでいる人々の顔を見るよう努めた。死者たちは宙に浮かんでかかとを生者の肩に載せて休め、一方生者たちは、愛撫しあっている —— というか並びながらもろにセックスをしている —— 二人の死者の体を次々通り抜けているが、誰も騒ぎ立てはしない。驚くべきことではあるまいか、普通の状況では死者と生者は実にうまくやっているのだ。たがいを無視しあっていられる限りは。
　アランは言った。「僕がよその女を見るのは、それは —— それは、たとえば誰か女が通りかかったら、ラヴィもあんなふうなのかなあって思うからさ。もしかしたらラヴィもあんなふうに早足で歩くのかもしれない。ラヴィのお尻も歩くとあんなふうに揺れるのかもしれない。知らな

she's walking. And when some woman laughs, I think maybe that's how Lavvie sounds when she laughs. I know Lavvie's hair is blonde. I find her hairs on the sheets sometimes, and in the ❶drain. She's told me that she has brown eyes. I know how tall she is. Sex. Ah, sex isn't very good right now, but sometimes I wake up in the middle of the night and I can feel her lying on top of me. She's so heavy! She's cold and she's real curvy and she doesn't breathe, but sometimes she coughs and coughs and can't stop. She just lies there on top of me, with her cheek on my cheek. And I think she's smiling, but I don't know why she's smiling. I don't know what she's smiling about. She won't tell me. She writes stuff on my skin with her finger, but I don't know what she's writing. Sometimes the kids get in bed too, and do you know what that's like, ❷rolling over and there are a couple of dead kids in bed with you? And Lavvie, I don't know if Lavvie ❸bounces when she walks, or if she ❹trips over things, or if she still thinks my jokes are funny, or if she even listens when I'm talking. If she's even there. Or if she just laughs at me when I'm yelling at her. I don't know when she's being ❺sarcastic or when I've really hurt her feelings or when she's teasing me. I know she's there, but she seems so far away. Sometimes when I come up to bed, I think maybe somebody else has been up there. Not one of the kids, or Lavvie, but somebody else. Some other dead person. He goes through my drawers and he throws stuff

---

❶drain: 排水口　❷roll(ing) over: 寝返りを打つ　❸bounce(s): 弾むように歩く　❹trip(s) over...: 〜につまずいてよろける　❺sarcastic: 皮肉な、嫌味な

い女が笑っても、ラヴィも笑うとあんな声なのかなあって思うんだ。ラヴィが金髪だってことはわかってる。時おりシーツや排水口に髪が落ちてるからね。瞳は茶色だって彼女から聞いた。背の高さもわかってる。セックス。うん、セックスは目下あんまり調子よくないけど、たまに、夜中に目が覚めると彼女が僕の上に乗っているのがわかるんだ。すごく重いんだよ！　冷たくて、すごくこうカーブしていて、息はしないけどときどきすごく咳込んで全然止まらなかったりする。僕の上でただ横になって、頬を僕の頬にくっつけているのさ。顔には笑みを浮かべていると思うんだけど、なんで微笑んでいるのかはわからない。いったい何があるんだろうね、微笑むことなんて。彼女は何も言わない。指で僕の体に字を書くんだけど、なんと書いているかはわからない。子供たちもベッドに入ってくることがあって、そういうのってどんな感じかわかるかい、こう、寝返りを打ったら死んでる子供が二人ばかり横にいるんだぜ。それでラヴィだけど、彼女が歩くときに弾むように歩くのか僕は知らないし、物につまずいたりするのか、僕のジョークをいまも面白いと思ってるのか、そもそも僕が喋ってるときにちゃんと聞いてるのかどうかも僕にはわからない。そもそも彼女がそこにいるかどうかも。僕がどなりつけてもあざ笑ってるだけかもしれないけどそれもわからない。きつい皮肉を言っていても、僕のふるまいに本気で傷ついていても、僕をからかっているだけだとしても、僕にはわからない。彼女がそこにいることはわかるけど、すごく遠くにいるような感じがする。時には、ベッドに行くと、誰かほかの人間がそこにいたように思えることもある。子供たちのうちの誰かじゃなくて、ラヴィでもなくて、誰かほかの人間が。誰かほかの死んだ人間が。そいつが僕のタンスをひっかき回して、

around. If it isn't Lavvie's boyfriend, then it's Lavvie or one of the kids. But they ❶swear up and down it isn't them, they say I'm imagining things. And then I think, so okay, even if you're really my kids, you're her kids, really. Because they're like her. They're just like her. They're dead too. So what I keep thinking is that this was a mistake right from the beginning. Like people say. Maybe the living shouldn't fall in love with the dead."

🎧073

Now Lavvie had come down out of the bougainvillea. She was curled up in her husband's lap, gazing up at him. Alan didn't seem to know she was there. Lavvie didn't say anything, she just winked at Sarah Parminter. It was ❷a furious wink. Isn't he a ❸card? Isn't he a ❹blabbermouth? He never shuts up, she said to Sarah. Talk, talk, talk. Let me tell you what I did today, Lavvie. Let me tell you what this guy said at work. Blah, blah, blah. Don't you just want to eat him up? If he leaves me, I'll make him wish he were dead, too.

🎧074

"What's she saying?" Alan said. "She's saying something to you, isn't she? Where is she? You can't believe a word she says. You think that just because you can hear her talking, just because you can see her, you think you know what she's thinking. You think

---

❶swear up and down (that) . . .: 〜と言い張る　❷a furious wink: ★直訳は「ものすごいウィンク」。　❸card: 変な奴　❹blabbermouth: おしゃべり

いろんな物をそこらへんにぶちまけるのさ。そいつがラヴィのボーイフレンドでないとしたら、やっぱりラヴィか子供の誰かかな。でもみんな絶対自分たちじゃないって言い張るのさ、パパの考え過ぎだよって。そう言われると僕もね、つい思ってしまうのさ、わかったよ、お前たちパパの子でもあるけどやっぱりママの子なんだなってね。だってあの子たち、彼女に似てるんだよ。何もかも似てるんだよ。やっぱり死んでるし。だから僕はどうしても思ってしまうのさ、この結婚はそもそものはじめから間違いだったんだって。世間で言う通りなんだな。生者は死者に恋をすべきじゃないんだよ」

　ラヴィはさっきブーゲンビリアから下りてきていた。いまは夫の膝の上で丸まって、彼をじっと見上げている。彼女がそこにいることがアランにはわかっていないようだった。ラヴィは何も言わず、セアラ・パーミンターにウィンクを送ってよこしただけだった。すごくはっきりしたウィンク。ねえ、この人ってすごくない？　すごくよく喋ると思わない？　絶対黙ってないのよね、と彼女はセアラに言った。べらべら、べらべら。なあラヴィ、今日ね、こんなことをやったんだぜ。会社でさ、こんなこと言った奴がいてさ。ぐだぐだぐだぐだぐだぐだ。もういっそこの人食べちゃいたくならない？　この人があたしを捨てたら、あいっそ俺も死んじまいたいって気にさせてやるわ。

　「なんて言ってるんだ？」とアランは言った。「あんたに何か言ってるんだろ？　どこにいるんだ、あいつは？　一言だって信じちゃ駄目だぜ、あいつの言うこと。あんたにはあいつの声が聞こえるから、あいつの姿が見えるから、あいつが何を考えてるかわかるって思うかもしれない。あいつがほんとのこと言ってるかどうかわかるって思うかもしれな

you can tell if she's telling the truth. But I've lived with her for the last twelve years and she's a liar and a bitch and she's a whore. Every time she opens that cold little mouth of hers, it's because she's thought up some new lie. Every time she says she loves me. If she could lie about death, if she could make people believe she was a living woman, she'd lie about that, too. Just because."

🎧075

The bougainvillea was getting thick with dead people. They hung down from the branches and listened to Alan. Lavvie listened hardest of all. Her face ❶shone with wifely approval.

"Alan," Sarah said. "Let's try to talk about this in a calm and reasonable manner."

🎧076

Recently, Sarah Parminter's clients had been coming to her, wanting her to fix their love lives. If you ❷read horoscopes, you'd think it was ❸something in the air. Perhaps someday soon the ❹alignment of the stars would change, all recent unhappinesses and catastrophes would be reversed and people would fall in love all over again and life would be good and death would be good too. Perhaps Sarah Parminter's own horoscope had advised her not to ❺meddle in other people's affairs at this time. But Sarah didn't believe in ❻astrology. Her cousin Fred was also a medium, and his clients were just as difficult, just as unhappy. Sarah and Fred some-

---

❶shone with wifely approval: ★直訳は「妻らしい賛同の表情で顔が輝いた」。　❷read horoscopes: 星占いをする　❸something in the air: ★直訳は「あたりに漂う何か」。　❹alignment: 配列　❺meddle in . . .: 〜にちょっかいを出す　❻astrology: 占星術

い。だけど僕はあいつと十二年間一緒に暮らしてきたんだ、あいつは嘘つきなんだ。嘘つきで、ろくでなしなのさ。あばずれなのさ。あの冷たい口を開くたび、また何か新しい嘘を思いついたのさ。僕のことを愛してるって言うたびにそうなのさ。もし死んでるってことについても嘘がつけて、自分は生きてる女なんだってみんなに信じ込ませることができるものなら、きっとその嘘もつくね。根っからの嘘つきなんだよ」

 ブーゲンビリアに死者たちが群がってきていた。みんな枝からぶら下がって、アランが喋るのを聞いている。ラヴィが一番熱心に聞いていた。妻らしい、夫を誇りに思う表情に瞳が輝いていた。

 「ねえアラン」とセアラは言った。「この話は落ち着いた、理性的なやり方で話すことにしましょうよ」

 このごろセアラ・パーミンターのところには、自分たちの愛の生活を立て直してもらいに客が訪れるようになっていた。星占いをする人間だったら、これも星のめぐりと関係があると思うかもしれない。じきに星々の配列も変わって、不幸も破綻も風向きが変わり、みんなまた恋に落ちて生は善きものとなり死も善きものとなるのだ、と。ひょっとすると、セアラ・パーミンター自身の星回りが、いまは他人の生活に干渉しないようにと告げていたのかもしれない。だがそもそもセアラは占星術を信じなかった。彼女のいとこのフレッドもやはり霊媒で、フレッドの顧客たちもやはり同じくらい扱いが厄介で同じくらい不幸だった。セア

times sat out on her balcony in the airless, dirty yellow afternoons, watching cars go up and down the ❶ramps of the I-5. They talked about work. Opposite the apartment building, there was a DEAD END sign across the street which someone had turned into DEAD ED. Every time she saw it, Sarah Parminter thought about going down and adding an FR. But Fred didn't have a great sense of humor. He claimed it had been ❷eroded away by contact with the other world. But Sarah remembered him as a child, and even then he'd never enjoyed the sort of ❸practical jokes that the dead liked to play.

🎧077

Fred had a new client, a man named Sam Callahan whose wife was also dead, just like Lavvie Tyler. Only the Callahans had been married for decades while both were still living, and the problem was now that she was dead, his wife didn't want to have anything to do with Sam Callahan. As far as she was concerned, the marriage was over. But Callahan couldn't ❹let go.

🎧078

Fred didn't approve of the way that Sarah ❺coddled her clients. When Callahan came in, what he'd said straightaway was, "I know who you want to talk to. But she doesn't want to talk to you."

Callahan was a big man with small hands. He said, "I was just hoping that I could talk to her one more time. I ❻fucked up. I'm sorry. I wanted to explain. I need to tell her how much I loved her.

---

❶ramps:（高速道路の出入り口の）傾斜路、ランプ　❷erode(d) away: 腐食する、浸食する
❸practical jokes: 悪戯、悪ふざけ　❹let go: 忘れる、あきらめる　❺coddle(d): 〜を甘やかす
❻fuck(ed) up: 台なしにする、しくじる

ラは時おり、風もない薄汚れた黄色い午後、フレッドと一緒にマンションのバルコニーに座って、Ｉ－5号線のランプを車が上り下りするのを眺めた。二人で仕事の話をした。マンションの向かいにDEAD END（行き止まり）と書かれた標識があって、誰かがそれをDEAD ED（死んでるエド）に直していた。それを見るたびセアラは、あそこへ行ってFRを書き足そうかと考えた。でもフレッドはユーモアのセンスがあるとは言いがたかった。あの字は来世との接触によって腐食したのだとフレッドは主張した。だがセアラは彼が子供だったころを覚えていた。子供のころからすでに、フレッドは死者たちがやりたがるたぐいの悪戯を楽しめる性格ではなかった。

　フレッドの新しい顧客で、サム・キャラハンという、妻がラヴィ・ロブリー＝タイラーと同じく死んでいる男がいた。ただしキャラハン夫妻の場合は、二人とも生きている時期に何十年も結婚生活を送っており、問題は、死者となったいま妻がサム・キャラハンといっさいかかわりを持ちたがっていないということだった。彼女にとって結婚はもう終わりだった。だが夫は別れたがらなかった。

　セアラが客を甘やかすのをフレッドはよくないと思っていた。キャラハンがやって来ると、フレッドは開口一番、「あなたが誰と話したいかはわかっています。でも向こうはあなたと話したがってませんよ」と言った。

　キャラハンは手の小さな大男だった。彼は言った。「あと一度だけ彼女と話せればと思ったんです。私は何もかも台なしにしてしまいました。後悔しています。すべてを説明したいんです。彼女をどれだけ愛していたか、言わずにはおれないんです。お願いですから、彼女が口をき

Please make her talk to me."

Fred said, "You do know she's dead, right?"

🎧079

There had been a boy at Callahan's school. Paul. That had been his name. After he did what he did, he still wasn't very popular, but he became more distinct. He came into focus.

The name of the girl he'd done it for: Popsicle. A nickname, because she was so cool.

🎧080

Everyone at school followed Popsicle around. Even the girls ❶had crushes on Popsicle. People gave her things. Sometimes ❷at recess there was an ice-cream truck parked across the street. Somebody bought Popsicle a cherry popsicle. Paul came back with six ice creams—a screwball, a popsicle, two creamsicles, a fudge pop, an ice-cream sandwich. He spent all his lunch money. His hands were full of ice cream. He went and stood in front of Popsicle. She said something like, I can't eat all those.

🎧081

Paul said, "I'll eat them for you. To prove how much I love you." As if they'd been arguing about it. Nobody even knew if he'd ever said anything to Popsicle before.

---

❶had crushes on . . .: 〜に夢中だった　❷at recess: 休み時間に

いてくれるよう取りもってください」
　フレッドは言った。「ちゃんとおわかりですよね、彼女がもう死んでいることは？」

　キャラハンが通っていた学校に、ある男の子がいた。ポール。それがその子の名前だった。あんなことをやったあとも、べつに人気者になりはしなかったが、前より目立つようになりはした。みんなの目が向くようになった。
　ポールはそれを、ポプシクルという女の子のためにやったのだった。「ポプシクル」はニックネームだ。何しろすごくクールな子だったのだ。
　学校じゅう、みんながポプシクルのことを追いかけ回した。女の子たちまでポプシクルに夢中だった。みんなが彼女にいろんな物をあげた。休み時間に、道路の向こう側にアイスクリーム・トラックが駐まっていることがあった。誰かがポプシクルにチェリー・ポプシクルアイスを買ってあげた。ポールはアイスクリームを六つ抱えて戻ってきた——スクルーボール、ポプシクル、クリームシクル二つ、ファジポップ、アイスクリーム・サンド。昼ご飯のお金を全部注ぎ込んだのだ。両手ともべたべたアイスクリームだらけだった。彼はポプシクルの前まで行って立ちどまった。そんなにたくさん食べきれないわ、とかなんとか彼女は言った。
　ポールは言った。「僕が食べてあげる。君をどれだけ愛しているか証明するために」。まるで、それまで二人で、彼がどれだけ彼女を愛しているかをめぐって言い争っていたみたいに。これまで彼が、ポプシクルに向かって一言でも喋ったことがあったかどうか、それすら誰も知らなかった。

🎧 082

All the other kids stood around and watched. Those who weren't there, who weren't watching, were pretty sure later on that they had been there: they'd heard the story so many times. Callahan thought he'd been there, although really he hadn't. When he fell in love for the first time, he remembered Paul's hands, Popsicle's polite, confused smile.

🎧 083

Later on, everybody watched Paul eat stuff, except for Popsicle, who hid in the girl's bathroom every single time. Nobody had crushes on her after a while. Nobody else loved her as much as Paul.

🎧 084

In his locker, Callahan had kept a list of everything Paul ate. It was a love poem, a grocery list, secret evidence: Paul loves Popsicle. Paul ate a few ants. He drank someone's milk, which had ❶gone off. Everyone smelled it. Paul ate a little glue booger that someone brought him. He ate dead leaves, and a ball of hair that someone took from Popsicle's comb. He ate a piece of raw meat a girl stole from her mother's refrigerator. He ate other things, all year long. The teachers never saw what was going on.

The next year Paul didn't come back. Neither did Popsicle. Someone made a joke about it. Perhaps Paul had eaten Popsicle.

---

❶ go(ne) off: 腐る

ほかの子供たちは周りに立って見守った。そこにいなかった子、見ていなかった子もみな、あとになると自分はそこにいたのだと思い込むようになった。それだけ何度も何度も話を聞いたのだ。自分もそこにいたとキャラハンも思っていたが、本当はいなかった。初めて恋に落ちたとき、キャラハンはポールの両手を思い出し、ポプシクルの儀礼的な、とまどいの混じった笑みを思い出した。
　そのあとの日々、ポールががつがつ食べるのをみんなが見物するようになった。でもポプシクルだけは、そのたびに女子トイレに隠れた。しばらくすると誰も彼女に夢中でなくなった。ポールほど彼女を愛している子はいなかった。
　キャラハンはロッカーに、ポールが食べたもののリストをしまっていた。それは愛の詩であり、買い物リストであり、秘密の証拠だった。ポールはポプシクルを愛している。ポールがアリを何匹か食べた。誰かの腐ったミルクを飲んだ。みんなに臭いがわかる腐り方だった。誰かが持ってきた小さな糊のかたまりをポールは食べた。枯れ葉を食べ、誰かがポプシクルの櫛から取ってきた髪の玉を食べた。ある女の子が家の冷蔵庫からくすねてきた生肉を一切れ食べた。一年じゅう、ほかにもいろんな物をポールは食べた。先生たちは全然気づかなかった。
　次の学年、ポールは戻ってこなかった。ポプシクルも戻ってこなかった。誰かが冗談を言った。ひょっとしてポールの奴、ポプシクルを食べちゃったんじゃないの。

🎧 085

Callahan didn't know what had happened to Paul or to Popsicle. Fred, on the other hand, knew what happens to everyone eventually. He could see the map that Paul and Popsicle had left on Callahan's face, just like Callahan's wife could see it now that she was dead. The dead can afford to see more than the living. Fred said, "She says you didn't really love her. And that she's ❶better off without you. She hopes you grow old and die alone."

🎧 086

Callahan said, "I'm paying you so you can say these things to me? This is bullshit! And how do I even know if she's really here? Why should I believe what some guy says? Why would she talk to you and not to me?"

Fred said, "Remember you're talking to a medium. Not a therapist." (He tried to ❷sound reasonable; ❸detached rather than snappish. He knew as he said it that he sounded like Callahan's therapist.) "Laura says you have more money than you know how to spend, and she says she hopes you spend it all on ❹charlatans and quacks. Don't get angry at me. I'm just saying this because you want me to tell you what she's saying."

🎧 087

Callahan said, "Laura, if you're here, talk to me—why are you talking to him, and not to me?" Like Fred, he was trying his best to talk reasonably. Soon he'd be throwing furniture around. "Don't

---

❶ better off without . . .: 〜がいない方が幸せで　❷ sound reasonable: 理性的な口調で話す、理にかなっているように聞こえる　❸ detached rather than snappish: 私情をはさまない (detached)、冷静な口調で　★snappishは「きつい言い方の」。　❹ charlatans and quacks: ペテン師やインチキ医者

ポールが、あるいはポプシクルがその後どうなったのかキャラハンは知らなかった。一方フレッドは、誰がいずれどうなるのか何もかも知っていた。ポールとポプシクルがキャラハンの顔に残していった地図がフレッドには見えた。死者となったいま、それはキャラハンの妻にも見えた。死者は生者より多くが見えるのだ。フレッドは言った。「あなたは彼女を本当に愛してはいなかったと彼女は言っています。あなたがいない方が幸せだと彼女は言っています。あなたが老いぼれて独りで死んでいけばいいと言っています」

　キャラハンは言った。「あんたにそんなこと言われるために俺は金を払ってるのか？　ふざけやがって！　だいたい彼女が本当にここにいるってどうやって俺にわかるんだ？　なんで他人の寝言なんか信じなくちゃならん？　なんで彼女が俺じゃなくてあんたとなら口をきくんだ？」

　フレッドは言った。「忘れないでください、いまあなたが話している相手は霊媒です。セラピストではありません」（理性的な口調で話そうとフレッドは努めた。私情をはさまない、冷静な口調。話しながら、自分がキャラハンのセラピストみたいな口調で喋っていることをフレッドは感じた）。「あなたには使いきれないくらいの金があるとローラは言っていて、全部ペテン師やインチキ医者に使ってしまえばいいと言っています。私に腹を立てないでくださいよ。私はただ、彼女がなんと言っているか、あなたがお聞きになりたがっているからお伝えしているだけなんですから」

　キャラハンは言った。「ローラ、そこにいるなら私と話しておくれ——なんでそんな奴と話して、私とは話さないんだ？」。フレッドと同じくキャラハンも理性的に話そうと頑張っている。じきに彼は家具を投

you know how much I love you?"

She knew. Even Fred knew. But what did how much matter to a dead woman?

🎧 088

Fred said, "She says you ought to take better care of yourself. Your refrigerator is empty. She wants you to go out and buy some groceries. She doesn't want you to ❶starve to death. She doesn't want to see you anytime soon. She's got her own afterlife to live, her own things to deal with. This is an important time for her. She has things to do."

🎧 089

"❷So is that it?" Callahan said. "Is that all you can do for me?"

Fred shrugged. "Do you want me to produce some ❸ectoplasm? A souvenir of the spirit world? Would you like to talk to somebody famous? Marilyn Monroe?"

"You are one real son of a bitch," Callahan said. "So how do you like the way this asshole talks to me, Laura? You approve?"

🎧 090

Fred said nothing. Laura said nothing, either. She indicated, however, that she'd like to write something down.

The table where they were sitting was solid oak. Round. No sharp edges. It was good to have a nice heavy piece of furniture to sit behind. Both the living and the dead liked to throw stuff around, as if it proved something. Fred kept a pad of paper and a

---

❶starve to death: 餓死する　❷(So) is that it?: それで終わりか？　❸ectoplasm: エクトプラズム　★霊媒の体から出るとされる超自然的物質。

げ飛ばしはじめるだろう。「君にはわからないのか、私が君を、どれだけ深く愛しているか？」

　もちろん彼女にはわかっている。フレッドにだってわかっている。だが死んでいる女性にとって、どれだけ深く、なんてことがどれだけ意味があるのか？

　フレッドは言った。「あなたはもっと体を大切にすべきだと彼女は言っています。家の冷蔵庫が空っぽでしょう。食料品を買いに出かけなさいと彼女は言っています。飢え死にしてほしくないと彼女は言っています。とうぶん顔を合わせたくないからと言っています。あたしにはあたしの来世があるんだしあたしなりにやるべきことがあるんだと彼女は言っています。いまは彼女にとって大事な時期なんです。彼女にはなすべきことがあるんです」

「それで終わりか？」とキャラハンは言った。「あんたにできるのはそれだけか？」

　フレッドは肩をすくめた。「何か心霊体でも出現させましょうか？ 霊界からのみやげ物でも？　誰か有名人とお話になりますか？　マリリン・モンロー？」

「底なしのクソ野郎」とキャラハンは言った。「なあローラ、お前このクソったれの話し方どう思う？　いいと思うか？」

　フレッドは何も言わない。ローラも何も言わない。ただし、何か書きたいという意思表示はした。

　彼らが座っているテーブルは、がっちりとしたオークだった。丸いテーブルで、どこも尖ったところはない。ずっしり重い家具を盾にできるのはありがたい。生者も死者も、やたらと物を投げたがるのだ。それ

ballpoint pen on the table. He picked the pen up so that Laura could write down exactly what she wanted to say. He didn't watch as Laura wrote. It was uncomfortable, watching someone else use your hand. The fingers always looked too ❶wriggly. Stretched. Laura dragged the pen across the page as if Fred's fingers were ❷bags of dirt.

🎧091

Callahan kept on talking to Laura. He had this feeling that Laura was hiding somewhere in the room, maybe under the medium's ❸floppy toupee, or under the oak table. Laura had never been good at keeping still. She liked to ❹swim laps until she could barely climb out of the pool. He couldn't help it. He said, "Do they have swimming pools? For dead people? Does Laura still swim every day?"

🎧092

Fred tried to keep a straight face. Swimming pools? He couldn't wait to tell that one to Sarah. "Yeah, sure," he said. "They have swimming pools. Laura's learning to play bridge. And she's thinking about getting a dog. You know, for companionship."

🎧093

Callahan thought about that. He could learn how to play bridge, if that was what Laura wanted. He was sure he could feel Laura moving around the room, brushing her fingers against the walls, sliding behind the curtains at the window, touching the backs of

---

❶wriggly: くねくね動く　❷bags of dirt: 土嚢　❸floppy toupee: へろへろの (floppy) かつら (toupee)　★toupeeは「(男性用の) 部分用かつら」。　❹swim laps: プールで何往復も泳ぐ　★lapは (水泳プールの) 1往復。

が何かの証(あか)しになるとでも思っているみたいに。フレッドはテーブルの上に、メモ用紙とボールペン一本を置いていた。言いたいことをローラがきっちり書けるようフレッドはペンを手にとった。ローラが書いているあいだ、フレッドは見ないようにした。他人が自分の手を使うのを見るのは気まずいものなのだ。いつ見ても、指はひどくくねくねに見える。でなければ妙にぴんとのびている。ローラはフレッドの指が土嚢(どのう)か何かであるみたいにずるずる引きずった。

　キャラハンはなおもローラに呼びかけた。ローラがこの部屋のどこかに隠れているのだ、霊媒のへろへろのかつらの下とかオークのテーブルの下とかに。ローラは昔からじっとしていられないたちだった。プールから這い上がるのもやっとになるまで泳ぐのが好きだった。キャラハンは訊かずにいられなかった。「死者はプールを持ってるのか？　死者のためのプールを？　ローラは毎日泳いでるのか？」

　フレッドは真顔を保つよう努めた。プール？　こいつはぜひセアラに聞かせてやらなくちゃ。「ええ、もちろん」と彼は言った。「ありますよ、プール。ローラはね、ブリッジも習っている最中です。犬も飼おうかと考えてるんです。伴侶にいいですからね、犬は」

　キャラハンはそう言われて考えた。ローラがそういうことを望むなら、自分もブリッジを習ってもいい。ローラが部屋のなかを動き回っているのがはっきりわかる気がした。指で壁をなぞったり、窓辺のカーテンの陰に身を滑り込ませたり、彼が腰かけている椅子の背に触れたり。

the chair where he sat, but Laura never touched him. What if she touched him and he couldn't feel anything? How was all this supposed to work, if they tried to make it work? They'd been married for almost thirty years.

🎧094

Fred read what Laura had written. Terrible handwriting, even for a dead person. "So she wants you to ❶throw a dinner party. But she doesn't want you to invite anyone else. This is the menu she's giving me. She says, you want to prove you love her, then prove it. Make her dinner."

Callahan said, "I used to make dinner for her all the time."

🎧095

Fred said, "You'll notice I haven't asked you why she's so mad at you. I'm not going to ask you, either. I don't like to ❷pry." He looked down at the list Laura was making, and then back up at Callahan. "But yeah, she's pretty ❸pissed. This is one ❹weird-ass menu. She says ants, a piece of churt—sorry, chalk, her handwriting is terrible—old milk, vinegar, popsicles, erasers, grass, sawdust, sand, dirt. She says if you really love her, you'll show her how much you love her."

🎧096

"So what did he do?" Sarah Parminter said, after a while. "Is he going to do it?"

"I don't know," Fred said. "I just thought it was kind of funny.

---

❶throw a dinner party: ディナーパーティを開く　❷pry: 詮索する　❸pissed: むかついた　❹weird-ass: おそろしく変な

でも絶対、彼には触れなかった。彼女が自分に触れて、何も感じられなかったら？　うまくやっていこうとするなら、どういうふうにやればいいのだろう？　三十年近く夫婦でいたのに。

　ローラがそこまで書いたことをフレッドは読んだ。いくら死者とはいえ、ものすごく下手な字だ。「ディナーパーティを開いてほしいとローラは言っています。でもほかには誰も呼ぶなと言っています。メニューはこうしてほしいと言っています。あたしを愛してると証明したいんならしてごらんなさい、あたしにディナーを作ってちょうだいと彼女は言っています」

　キャラハンは言った。「俺は年じゅう彼女にディナーを作っていたんだ」

　フレッドは言った。「おわかりでしょうが、彼女がなぜあなたにそんなに腹を立てているのか、私はお訊ねしていません。そういうことをうかがうつもりはないんです。詮索する気はありませんから」。ローラが書いている最中のリストを彼は見下ろし、それからまた顔を上げてキャラハンの方を向いた。「でも、そうなんです、けっこう怒ってるんです。ずいぶん変わったメニューだなあ。蟻数匹。チャートひとかけ ── 失礼、チョークだ、何しろすさまじい筆蹟でして ──、古くなったミルク、酢、ポプシクル、消しゴム、草、おがくず、砂、土。ほんとに愛してるんだったらどれだけ愛しているか見せてもらおうじゃないのと言っています」

　「で、どうしたの？」としばらくあとにセアラ・パーミンターは訊いた。「ほんとに作る気なわけ？」

　「知らない」とフレッドは答えた。「ちょっと面白いと思っただけだか

He wrote me a check and it ❶bounced. And she said he had lots of money too, so maybe it wasn't really his wife, even. Maybe it was just somebody who wanted to ❷fuck with him. I wouldn't eat grass just for a dead girl. Not unless she was paying me."

🎧 **097**

"You haven't mentioned your mother yet," Sarah Parminter said to Alan Robley.

"Why?" Alan said. "Is she here? Does she want to talk to me?"

"She's over there with the kids," Sarah said. "They're teasing a Goofy."

🎧 **098**

"She's good with the kids," Alan said. But he didn't look over to where a crowd was gathering around the Goofy. He wasn't going to tell his kids to leave the Goofy alone. Living parents had a hard time disciplining dead children. You had to ❸indulge them, even when their fun got a little ❹vicious. You had to pretend that they didn't belong to you. "I mean, even when she was alive, she was good with them. She was so excited to have grandchildren. She read to them all the time."

🎧 **099**

"She didn't like Lavvie much," Sarah said.

"No," Alan said. "They didn't get along."

"Your mother still doesn't approve," Sarah said. "She still thinks

---

❶bounce(d): 不渡りになって戻ってくる　❷fuck with . . .: 〜を困らせる　★この語は使用を避けるべき。　❸indulge: 〜を甘やかす、〜の好き勝手にさせる　❹vicious: 悪意のある、意地悪な

らさ。支払いは小切手を渡されたんだけど、不渡りで戻ってきた。すごい金持ちだって女の方は言ってたのにな。ひょっとすると、妻なんかじゃなくて赤の他人だったのかもしれない。誰かが奴をとっちめてやろうと思っただけかも。死んだ女のために草を食うなんて僕は御免だな。金ももらわずにそんなことするなんて」

　「お母さまのお話をまだうかがってませんわ」とセアラ・パーミンターはアラン・ロブリー=タイラーに言った。
　「どうして？」とアランは言った。「お袋もここにいるんですか？　僕と話したがってるんですか？」
　「あっちの方に、子供たちと一緒にいらっしゃいます」とセアラは言った。「みんなでグーフィをからかってます」
　「お袋は子供の相手が上手なんだ」とアランは言ったが、グーフィの周りに人だかりができかけているあたりを見ようとはしなかった。グーフィに構うんじゃない、と子供たちに言うつもりもなかった。生きている親が死んでいる子供をしつけるのは大変なのだ。悪ふざけが多少度を超しても、甘い顔をせざるをえない。自分の子ではないふりをするしかないのだ。「いやつまり、生きてるあいだも子供の相手が上手だったってことです。孫ができてものすごく喜んでましたから。年じゅうおはなしを読んで聞かせてましたよ」
　「ラヴィのことは、そんなに気に入っていらっしゃらなかったですよね」とセアラは言った。
　「ええ」とアランは言った。「あんまり仲はよくなかった」
　「お母さまはいまだに認めてらっしゃらないんです」とセアラは言っ

Lavvie's too old for you."

Lavvie said something.

"Lavvie says your mother is a real, ah, bitch."

🎧 100

"Fuck Lavvie," Alan said, but he didn't really mean it. And now he was watching the Goofy ❶stumble around, and he was feeling an odd jealousy. Here he was, all dressed up in red, and the kids still preferred a guy in a fur suit to their own father. Dead people had favorite characters at Disneyland. Goofy, for example. The costume was so ❷baggy. That silly hat. You could ❸poke him in the ass, really jab him good, and he never moved fast enough. Minnie Mouses were also popular with dead people. They liked hiding her pocketbook. Or putting things in it.

🎧 101

The Goofy was shouting ❹obscenities now. Living children were crying. Dead ones were laughing. Alan said, "She never made any effort. She always made fun of my mother, the way she put on lipstick, and why are the dead so ❺obsessed with makeup, anyway? The way my mother cut up her food real small."

🎧 102

Lavvie said something else.

"Lavvie wants to know if you ever loved her," Sarah said. It delighted her, how the line for Space Mountain never got any shorter,

---

❶stumble around: よたよた歩き回る ❷baggy: だぶだぶの ❸poke . . . in the ass: 〜の尻をつつく ❹obscenities: 卑猥な言葉 ❺obsessed with . . .: 〜にとりつかれた

た。「ラヴィはあなたには年上すぎるといまだに思ってらっしゃるんです」

　ラヴィが何か言った。

「ラヴィが言っています。あなたのお母さんはほんとに、あの、クズだって」

「ラヴィこそクズだ」とアランは言ったが、本気ではなかった。そしていま、グーフィがよたよた歩き回るのを眺めながら、彼は奇妙な嫉妬を感じていた。こっちはこうやってちゃんと赤ずくめの格好をしてるのに、子供たちは実の父親より毛皮の着ぐるみをかぶった奴の方がいいなんて。ディズニーランドには死者好みのキャラクターがいろいろいる。たとえばグーフィがそうだ。あのだぼだぼのコスチュームがいいのか。あの間抜けな帽子とか。尻をつついても思いきりこづいても、絶対すばやく動いたりしないからやりたい放題。ミニーマウスも死者に人気だ。ミニーのハンドバッグを隠すことを死者たちは好む。あるいはバッグのなかに何か入れるとか。

　グーフィが卑猥な言葉をわめき散らしている。生きている子供たちは泣いていた。死んでいる子たちは笑っていた。アランは言った。「全然歩み寄ろうとしなかったんだ。いつもお袋のことをからかってばかりで。口紅のつけ方とかそういうことを —— だいたいなんで死者たちはあんなに化粧にこだわるんだ？　あと、お袋が食べ物をすごく細かく刻むこととか」

　ラヴィがまた何か言った。

「あなた私を一度でも愛したことがあるのかしらってラヴィが言ってます」とセアラは言った。〈スペース・マウンテン〉の列がいつまでも短

no matter how long you sat and watched. She'd never waited, herself. It was enough to watch the tourists ❶shuffle into line, disappear and come back out again, and wander over to join the line once again.

🎧103

"Could I talk to my mom?" Alan said.

Sarah tried waving Alan's mother over, but Mrs. Robley only gave her ❷a black, murderous glare. Her lips were pressed together so tightly that her entire mouth had disappeared. One hand was ❸clamped around the Goofy's long ear. The other hand was ❹burrowing into the Goofy's costume, as if she were going to ❺disembowel him right through the fake fur. Lavvie was still sitting weightlessly in Alan's lap. The little ❻slut. She ❼gave Mrs. Robley the finger when the kids weren't looking.

"She's, ah, she's busy," Sarah said. "And our time's up, Alan. I have another appointment at four. But Lavvie has one last thing to say to you."

🎧104

Lavvie didn't really have anything to say to Alan, but Sarah knew she wouldn't mind that Sarah was making something up. The stranger the better: it would only amuse her. All of it was true, after all. I love you. I don't love you. Don't leave me. Fuck off. I fuck the ghost of ❽Eleanor Roosevelt with a ❾dildo all day long while you're at work.

---

❶shuffle into . . .: ぞろぞろと〜に入る　★shuffleは「足を引きずって歩く」。　❷a black, murderous glare: 陰険な（black）、悪意のこもった（murderous）目　★glareは「睨みつけること」。　❸clamp(ed): 締めつける　❹burrow(ing) into . . .: 〜の中に潜り込む　❺disembowel: 〜の内臓を抜く　❻slut: ふしだらな女　★侮蔑的な語。　❼gave Mrs. Robley the finger: ミセス・ロブリーに向けて卑猥なジェスチャーを送った　★give 人 the fingerは「（人に）中指をつき立てる」しぐさで、ひじょうに侮蔑的なジェスチャーとされる。　❽Eleanor Roosevelt: ★米国第32代大統領フランク

くならないのがセアラには嬉しかった。いくら長いあいだ見ていても、絶対に短くならない。自分で並んだことは一度もなかった。観光客たちがぞろぞろと列に入っていって、中に消え、また出てきて、もう一度ふらふら列に入っていくのを見るだけで十分だった。

「お袋と話させてもらえますか？」とアランは言った。

セアラは手を振ってアランの母親を呼びよせてみたが、ミセス・ロブリーは陰険な、悪意のこもった目で睨み返しただけだった。唇はぎゅっときつく閉ざされ、口がすっかり消えてしまっている。片手はグーフィの長い耳をしっかりつかんでいる。もう一方の手はグーフィのコスチュームのなかをごそごそかき回していた。にせの毛皮の奥に手をつっ込んで、内臓をえぐり出してやろうとでも思っているみたいな勢いだ。ラヴィは相変わらず、重みのない体でアランの膝の上に座っている。このあばずれが。ラヴィもラヴィで、子供たちがよそを向いたすきを狙って、ミセス・ロブリーに向けて卑猥なジェスチャーを送った。

「ええと、いまはちょっと、忙しいみたい」とセアラは言った。「それに私、もう今日は時間ですから。四時に別のお客様とお約束がありますもので。でもラヴィが最後にもう一言だけと言ってます」

ラヴィはもうアランに言うことなんか何もなかったが、セアラが何かでっち上げても彼女が気にしないだろうとセアラは見抜いていた。どうせならとことん変なことを言った方がいい。その方が面白がってもらえる。それに何を言おうと、結局は真実なのだ。愛してるわ。愛してないわ。私を捨てないで。ファックオフ。あんたが仕事してるあいだあたしは一日じゅう張形(はりがた)でエリノア・ローズベルトの幽霊にファックしてるのよ。

リン・D・ローズベルト（1882-1945）の夫人。社会運動家。　❾dildo: 張形(はりがた)

If Alan divorced Lavvie, he'd still need Sarah. There would be issues of child ❶custody. And there was Mrs. Robley, too. There would be things Alan needed to ask his mother about his childhood.

A divorce would mean more trips to amusement parks for the kids and for Sarah. She could always say the kids wanted to go to Six Flags next week. There were always good lines for the Psyclone.

🎧 105

Alan was still waiting, his hands in his lap. Let him wait a minute longer. It was strange, the way his arms just disappeared right through Lavvie's body. And it was unkind of Lavvie, Sarah thought, to sit like that. It was ❷indecent and unkind. Someday she might write an etiquette book for the dead, although it would be the living that ❸ended up reading it, no doubt, and one ought to draw a veil over certain things. Or at least not pull the veil back too far. Sarah had talked to a historian once—had he been a living man or had he already been dead? He was certainly dead now—about the past. The past was, of course, a different country. A different amusement park and the lines were much longer. The dead didn't know ❹the way back any better than the living did.

🎧 106

Sarah's historian said that one way you ❺went about figuring out what the past had been like was to read ❻contemporary books of etiquette. When one of these etiquette books suggested that it was

---

❶custody: 親権、養育権　❷indecent: 見苦しい、下品な　❸end(ed) up . . .ing: 結局〜する羽目になる　❹the way back: はるか昔　❺went about figuring out: ★go about . . .は「(仕事など)に取り組む」、figure out . . .は「(答えなど)を割り出す」。　❻contemporary: 同時代の、当時の

もしアランがラヴィと離婚しても、セアラの協力はその後も必要だろう。子供の養育権問題があるし、ミセス・ロブリーのこともある。自分の子供のころについて、母親に訊いておきたい事柄も出てくるだろう。
　離婚となれば、子供たちもセアラも、まだ何べんか遊園地へ来られるだろう。子供たちが来週シックス・フラッグズへ行きたいと言ってます、とセアラが言えば事足りる。〈サイクロン〉の前にも、いつもいい感じの行列ができている。
　アランは両手を膝に置いて、なおも待っている。もうしばらく待たせておこう。アランの両腕が、ラヴィの体のなかにすっと消えているのは妙な眺めだった。でもずっとこんなふうに座ってるなんて、さすがにラヴィは薄情すぎないだろうか、とセアラは思った。見苦しいし、薄情だ。いつの日か、死者のためのエチケット・ブックを書こうか。でもどうせ読むのは生者だろうし、ベールを掛けておいた方がいい物事もある。少なくとも、ベールをあまり派手に引っぱり上げない方がいい。セアラは以前、ある歴史家と ── あの人は生者だっただろうか、それとももう死んでいたか？　いまはもう間違いなく死んでいるだろう ── 過去について話しあったことがある。過去とは、言うまでもなく、よその国である。よその遊園地であり、列はここよりずっと長い。昔については、死者だってべつに生者以上に詳しくはない。
　セアラの話した歴史家は、過去がどんなだったかを知るひとつの手は、当時のエチケット本を読むことだと言った。たとえばそういう本に、道端の溝から人間のウンコを拾い上げてその色や大きさについてあ

not ❶well-bred behavior to pick up ❷a human turd from the gutter to ❸remark upon its color or size, you knew then that people had needed to be told not to do such things because they'd once done such things. Sarah ❹hadn't batted an eye when he'd said that. Better not to ❺let on about the habits of the dead, she knew. Sarah knew this, and Lavvie Tyler and the Robley-Tyler children and Mrs. Robley know this, and me, I know, too. Even as I've been telling you this story, I haven't described things exactly as they went on. I haven't been honest about the dead people in this story, about how the dead ❻carry on.

🎧 107

There were living people waiting in line at Disneyland, and there was a dead woman sitting on the park bench with Sarah Parminter and Alan Robley and there were lots of other dead people, too, hundreds of them, and ❼what they got up to isn't any of your business. ❽It's just as well that only people like Sarah Parminter and her cousin Fred ever see what the dead are really like. But the dead, of course, see everything that you do. Next time you and your new wife take your kids to Disneyland and you're waiting in line, you think about me. You think about that.

---

❶well-bred: 育ちのよい、上品な ❷a human turd: 人糞 ❸remark upon . . .: ～について口にする ❹not bat(ted) an eye: 顔色一つ変えない、動じない ❺let on about . . .: ～について漏らす ❻carry on: 好き放題にふるまう ❼what they got up to: 彼らが何をしでかしたか ★get up to . . .は「（いたずらなど）をしでかす」(p.72と同じ使い方)。 ❽It's just as well that . . .: ～してよかったくらいだ

れこれ言うのは上品な行ないではありませんと書いてあったら、それはかつて人々がそういうことをしていて、そうしないよう言われる必要があったということだ。歴史家がそう言ったとき、セアラは少しも動じなかった。死者の習慣についても、あんまり詳しく知らせない方がいい。セアラはそのことを知っていたし、ラヴィ・ロブリー＝タイラーもロブリー＝タイラー家の子供たちもミセス・ロブリーも知っているし、そして私——私も知っている。こうしてあなたにこの話を語ってきた私だが、いろんなことを起きたとおり正確に語ってはいない。この話の死者たちについて、死者たちのふるまいについて、正直に語ってはいないのだ。

　ディズニーランドでは生者たちが列を作って並び、ベンチには死んでいる女が一人、セアラ・パーミンターとアラン・ロブリー＝タイラーとともに座っていた。そしてほかにも死人が何百といたのであり、彼らが何をしでかしたかはあなたの知ったことではないのだ。セアラ・パーミンターやそのいとこのフレッドのような人だけが死者の真の姿を見られるというのは、むしろ幸いというべきだろう。だがむろん、死者の方は、あなたのやっていることを何から何まで見ている。今度新しい奥さんと一緒に、子供たちをディズニーランドに連れていって、列に並んで待つことになったら、私のことを考えてほしい。ちょっと考えてみてほしい。

Story 4
🎧 108-122

PET MILK
by
Stuart Dybek
ペット・ミルク
スチュアート・ダイベック

　安物のコーヒーミルクがカップのなかで描く渦と、外の雲が描く渦とが書き出しにおいて重ねあわされ、さらにそれが、恋人とレストランで飲むリキュールに浮かぶクリームの渦へとつながっていく。こうした広がり方が、この作品全体の（そしてほかのダイベック作品にもあてはまる）空間的・時間的広がりを代表している。
　心のなかではいまだ旧世界に住んでいるように思える祖母のラジオからは、ヨーロッパのさまざまな国からの放送が混じりあう。電車のなかで抱きあう若者とその恋人の姿を、かつての若者自身であるかのような高校生が見て、あたかも未来の自分に挨拶を送るかのように手を振る。いま・ここはいろんな形でいま以外・ここ以外とつながっている。
　このような時空間上の「風通しのよさ」がダイベックの小説の大きな魅力だが、といってもそれは、人間が自由であってどこへでも行けて何でもできるという単純な楽観につながりはしない。この「ペット・ミルク」でも、恋人同士が将来の夢を語りあうのを聞くなかで、逆に我々は、彼らがいずれたがいから離れてしまうことを予感する。風通しのよさにはいつも、喪失の影がさしているのである。

🎧 108

 Today I've been drinking instant coffee and Pet milk, and watching it snow. It's not that I enjoy the taste especially, but I like the way ❶Pet milk swirls in the coffee. Actually, my favorite thing about Pet milk is ❷what the can opener does to the top of the can. The can is unmistakable—compact, seamless looking, its very shape suggesting that it could condense milk ❸without any trouble. The can opener bites in neatly, and the thick liquid spills from the ❹triangular gouge ❺with a different look and viscosity than milk. Pet milk isn't real milk. The color's ❻off, to start with. There's almost something of the past about it, like old ivory. My grandmother always drank it in her coffee. When friends ❼dropped over and sat around the kitchen table, my grandma would ask, "Do you take cream and sugar?" Pet milk was the cream.

🎧 109

 There was a yellow plastic radio on her kitchen table, ❽usually tuned to the polka station, though sometimes she'd ❾miss it by half a notch and get the Greek station instead, or the Spanish, or the Ukrainian. In Chicago, where we lived, all the ❿incompatible states of Europe were pressed together down ⓫at the staticky right end of the dial. She didn't seem to notice, as long as she wasn't hearing English. The radio, turned low, played constantly. Its top was warped and turning amber on the side where the ⓬tubes were. I remember the sound of it on winter afternoons after school, as I sat

---

❶ Pet milk swirls in the coffee: ペット・ミルクがコーヒーのなかで渦を描く　★Pet milkは無糖のコンデンス・ミルクの商標。　❷ what the can opener does to the top of the can: ★直訳すれば「缶切りが缶の表面に対してなすこと」。　❸ without any trouble: 楽々と、難なく　❹ triangular gouge: 三角の溝　❺ with a different look and viscosity than milk: ミルクとは見かけも粘りも違う　❻ off: 外れている、ずれている　❼ drop(ped) over: 立ち寄る　❽ usually tuned to the polka station: だいたいいつもポルカ専門の局に合わせてあった　★polkaはボヘミア（現チェコ）

僕は今日、雪が降るのを眺めながら、ペット・ミルクを入れたインスタントコーヒーを飲んでいる。べつに味が素晴らしいからではない。ペット・ミルクがコーヒーのなかで渦を描くのを見るのが好きなのだ。そもそもペット・ミルクでいちばん好きなのは、缶切りを缶の表面に食い込ませる瞬間だ。缶自体も独特である──コンパクトで、表面には継ぎ目も見えず、形からしていかにもミルクを濃縮しそうだ。缶切りがその刃をすうっと食い込ませると、どろっとした液体が三角の溝からこぼれ出る。それはミルクとは見かけも粘りも違う液体だ。ペット・ミルクは本物のミルクではない。まず色からして冴えない。何となく、古い象牙のように、過ぎた昔を思わせるところがある。僕の祖母はコーヒーにかならずペット・ミルクを入れて飲んでいた。知りあいの人たちがうちに寄って、台所のテーブルに集まるたびに、祖母はいつも「クリームとお砂糖は入れる？」と訊いた。クリームというのはペット・ミルクのことだった。

　祖母の台所のテーブルには、黄色いプラスチック製のラジオがあった。だいたいいつもポルカ専門の局に合わせてあったが、時おりダイヤルを目盛り半分くらい合わせそこなって、代わりにギリシャ語の局や、スペイン語、ウクライナ語の局が聞こえてきたりした。僕らが住んでいたシカゴでは、ヨーロッパじゅうの、相容れないいくつもの国家が、雑音の多いダイヤル右端のあたりに一緒くたに詰め込まれていた。英語が聞こえてこないかぎり、祖母には気にならないみたいだった。ラジオは低い音量でいつもかならず鳴っていた。ボディの上部は歪み、側面も真空管付近が琥珀色に変わりかけていた。冬の午後に、学校から帰ってき

生まれの大衆的な舞踊・舞曲のこと。ダイベックの短篇は、東欧系の移民の多いシカゴの下町がしばしば舞台となる。　❾ miss it by half a notch: ダイヤルを目盛り半分くらい合わせそこなって　❿ incompatible: 相容れない、共存できない　⓫ at the staticky right end of the dial: 雑音の多い（staticky）ダイヤル右端のあたりに　⓬ tubes: 真空管

by her table watching the Pet milk swirl and cloud in the steaming coffee, and noticing, outside her window, the sky doing the same thing above the railroad yard across the street.

🎧 110

And I remember, much later, seeing the same swirling sky in tiny liqueur glasses containing a drink called a King Alphonse: the crème de cacao rising like smoke in repeated explosions, blooming in kaleidoscopic clouds through the layer of heavy cream. This was in the Pilsen, a little Czech restaurant where my girlfriend, Kate, and I would go sometimes in the evening. It was the first year out of college for both of us, and we had astonished ourselves by finding real jobs—no more waitressing or pumping gas, the way we'd done in school. I was ❶investigating credit references at a bank, and she was doing ❷something slightly above the rank of typist for Hornblower & Weeks, the investment firm. My bank showed training films that emphasized the importance of suitable dress, good ❸grooming, and personal neatness, even for employees like me, who worked at the switchboard in the basement. Her firm ❹issued directives on appropriate attire—skirts, for instance, should cover the knees. She had lovely knees.

🎧 111

Kate and I would sometimes meet after work at the Pilsen,

---

❶ investigating credit references: 信用照会状の調査に携わって　★「信用照会」とは、申込人のクレジットの履歴や現在のクレジットの利用状況を個人信用情報機関に問い合わせること。
❷ something slightly above the rank of typist: タイピストよりわずかに格が上の仕事
❸ grooming: 身だしなみ　❹ issued directives on appropriate attire: 勤務に適した服装に関する指示を出していた

て聞いたラジオの音を僕は思い出す。祖母のテーブルの前に座ってそれを聞きながら、湯気を立てているコーヒーのなかでペット・ミルクが渦を巻き、雲のような模様を描くのを僕は見つめるのだった。ふと窓の外に目をやると、通りの向かいの鉄道操車場の上で、空も同じことをやっていた。
　そして僕は、ずっとあとになって、それと同じ渦巻く空を、小さなリキュールグラスのなかに見たことを思い出す。グラスにはキング・アルフォンスと呼ばれるドリンクが入っていた。クレーム・ド・カカオがぼっぼっと煙のようにくり返し立ちのぼり、とろっとしたクリームの層をつき破って、万華鏡を思わせる華やかな雲を開かせるのだ。それを見たのは、ピルセンという小さなチェコ料理屋でのことだった。僕は時どきそこへ、ガールフレンドのケイトと一緒に夕食に出かけたのだ。二人とも大学を出て最初の年だった。本物の仕事が見つかって、僕らは自分でもびっくりしていた。もう学生のころみたいに、ウェイトレスやガソリンスタンドのアルバイトに明け暮れなくていいのだ。僕は銀行に就職して、信用照会状を調査する仕事をしていた。ケイトは投資会社のホーンブロウアー＆ウィークスで、タイピストよりわずかに格が上の仕事をしていた。僕は研修用の映画を何本も見せられた。適切な服装、きちんとした身だしなみ、清潔さの習慣等々の重要性を説く映画である。僕みたいに地下の交換台で働く連中にまでそういうことを教え込むのだ。ケイトの会社には、勤務に適した衣服に関する内規があった。たとえば、スカートは膝が隠れる長さがなくてはならない。ケイトは素敵な膝をしていた。
　ケイトと僕は時どき、仕事が終わったあとピルセンで待ちあわせた。

dressed in our proper business clothes and still feeling both a little self-conscious and glamorous, as if we were ❶impostors wearing disguises. The place had small, round oak tables, and we'd sit in a corner under a painting called "The Street Musicians of Prague" and trade future plans as if they were escape routes. She talked of going to ❷grad school in Europe; I wanted to apply to ❸the Peace Corps. Our plans for the future made us laugh and feel close, but those same plans somehow made anything more than temporary between us seem impossible. It was the first time I'd ever had the feeling of missing someone I was still with.

🎧112

 The waiters in the Pilsen wore short black jackets over long white aprons. They were old men from the old country. We went there often enough to have our own special waiter, Rudi, a name he pronounced with a rolled *R*. Rudi ❹boned our trout and seasoned our salads, and at the end of the meal he'd bring the bottle of crème de cacao from the bar, along with two little glasses and a small pitcher of heavy cream, and make us each a King Alphonse right at our table. We'd watch as he'd fill the glasses halfway up with the syrupy brown liqueur, then carefully attempt to float a layer of cream on top. If he failed to float the cream, we'd get that one free.

---

 ❶impostors wearing disguises: 変装したペテン師 ❷grad school: 大学院 ★graduate school の 略。 ❸the Peace Corps: 平 和 部 隊 ★Corpsは[kɔːr]と 読 む。 ❹boned our trout and seasoned our salads: 鱒の骨を抜いてくれたり、サラダにドレッシングをかけてくれたりした

二人ともまだ仕事用のきちんとした服を着ていて、何となく気恥ずかしいような、と同時に何だかすごく偉くなったような気持ちがした。変装したペテン師みたいな気分だった。店には小さな丸い樫のテーブルがいくつもあった。僕らは隅っこの、「プラハの街頭音楽師たち」と題する絵の下のテーブルに座り、将来の計画を、まるで逃走経路でも相談するみたいに話しあうのだった。ヨーロッパの大学院に留学しようかな、と彼女は言った。平和部隊に入りたい、と僕は言った。そういう話をするとき、僕たちはよく笑った。たがいにとても親密な気持ちになった。でも、まさにそういう計画ゆえに、僕たちは一時的以上の関係には絶対になれない気もした。こうしてケイトと一緒にいるのに、僕はもう彼女がいなくなって寂しいような気分を味わっていた。ケイト以外の女の子に、こんな気持ちになったことは一度もなかった。
　ピルセンのウェイターは、長い白のエプロンをつけて、その上に短めの黒い上着を着ていた。彼らは旧世界から来た年配の男たちだった。何べんか通（かよ）ったおかげで、僕らには馴染みのウェイターができていた。ルーディという名で、本人はそのRを巻き舌で発音した。ルーディは鱒の骨を抜いてくれたり、サラダにドレッシングをかけてくれたりした。そして食事が終わると、バーからクレーム・ド・カカオのボトルを持ち出し、小さなグラスを二つと、濃いクリームの入った小さなピッチャーと一緒にテーブルに運んできて、その場で僕らにキング・アルフォンスを一杯ずつ作ってくれた。僕らに見守られながら、ルーディはシロップのような茶色いリキュールをグラスの半分あたりまで入れ、それから、慎重な手付きで、その上にクリームの膜を浮かせようとした。もしクリームがうまく浮かなかったら、その一杯はただになるのだ。

🎧 113

"Who was King Alphonse anyway, Rudi?" I sometimes asked, trying to break his concentration, and if that didn't work I ❶nudged the table with my foot so the glass would ❷jiggle imperceptibly just as he was floating the cream. We'd usually ❸get one on the house. Rudi knew what I was doing. In fact, serving the King Alphonses had been his idea, and he had also suggested ❹the trick of jarring the table. I think it pleased him, though he seemed concerned about the way I'd stare into the liqueur glass, watching the patterns.

"It's not a microscope," he'd say. "Drink."

He liked us, and we tipped extra. It felt good to be there and to be able to pay for a meal.

🎧 114

Kate and I met at the Pilsen for supper on my twenty-second birthday. It was May, and unseasonably hot. I'd opened my tie. Even before looking at the dinner menu, we ordered a bottle of Mumm's and a dozen oysters ❺apiece. Rudi ❻made a sly remark when he brought the oysters on platters of ice. They were freshly opened and smelled of the sea. I'd heard people ❼joke about oysters being aphrodisiac but never considered it anything but a myth—the kind of idea they still had in the old country.

---

❶ nudge(d) the table with my foot: 片足でテーブルをそっと揺する　❷ jiggle imperceptibly: わずかに揺れる　❸ get one on the house: 一杯は店のおごりになる　★on . . .で「〜のおごりで」。 ❹ the trick of jarring the table: テーブルを揺らすというアイデア　❺ apiece: それぞれ　★=each　❻ made a sly remark: 思わせぶりのジョークを言った　★slyは「裏の意味があるような」。 ❼ joke about oysters being aphrodisiac: 牡蠣が媚薬だということをネタにした冗談を言う　★aphrodisiacは「催淫性の、性欲を促す」。

PET MILK by Stuart Dybek

「ねえ、そもそもキング・アルフォンスって誰なの、ルーディ？」と僕は時おり、彼の集中力を妨げようとして訊いた。それでもだめだと、ルーディがまさにクリームを浮かせようとする瞬間に、片足でテーブルをそっと揺すって、グラスをわずかに動かそうとした。たいてい一杯は店のおごりになった。ルーディも僕の悪戯を承知していた。そもそもキング・アルフォンスを作るというのはルーディの思いつきだったし、テーブルを揺らすというアイデアも彼のほうから仄めかしたのだ。たぶん彼も楽しんでいたのだと思う。もっとも、僕がリキュール・グラスをじっと睨みつけ、飲み物が描く模様を凝視しているのを見ると、ちょっと不安そうな顔をした。

「顕微鏡じゃないんだよ」と彼は言った。「飲みなさい」

ルーディは僕たちのことが気に入っていた。僕たちもチップを余分にあげた。ピルセンにいるのはいい気持ちだった。ちゃんとした食事をするお金があるのはいい気持ちだった。

　僕の二十二歳の誕生日に、僕らはピルセンで待ちあわせた。五月の、季節外れに暑い日で、僕はネクタイをほどいていた。ディナーのメニューも見ないうちから、僕らはマムズのボトルを一本取り、牡蠣を一ダースずつ注文した。氷に載った牡蠣を持ってきたルーディが、思わせぶりのジョークを言った。牡蠣は開けたてで、海の匂いがした。牡蠣が媚薬だということをネタにした冗談は前にも聞いたことがあったが、そんなのはどうせ神話だろうと僕は思っていた。旧世界でいまだに信じられている迷信のたぐいだろうと思ったのだ。

🎧 115

We squeezed on lemon, added ❶dabs of horseradish, slid the oysters into our mouths, and then rinsed the shells with champagne and drank the salty, cold juice. There was a beefy-looking couple eating ❷schnitzel at the next table, and they stared at us ❸with the repugnance that public oyster-eaters in the Midwest often encounter. We laughed and ❹grandly sipped it all down. I ❺was already half tipsy from drinking too fast, and starting to feel filled with ❻a euphoric, aching energy. Kate raised a ❼brimming oyster shell to me in a toast: "To the Peace Corps!"

"To Europe!" I replied, and we clunked shells.

She touched her wineglass to mine and whispered, "Happy birthday," and then suddenly leaned across the table and kissed me.

🎧 116

When she sat down again, she ❽was flushed. I ❾caught the reflection of her face in the glass-covered "The Street Musicians of Prague" above our table. I always loved seeing her in mirrors and windows. The reflections of her beauty startled me. I had told her that once, and she seemed to ❿fend off the compliment, saying, "That's because you've learned what to look for," as if it were a secret I'd stumbled upon. But, this time, seeing her reflection hovering ghostlike upon an imaginary Prague was like seeing a future from which she had vanished. I knew I'd never meet anyone more beautiful to me.

---

❶dabs of . . .: 少量の　❷schnitzel: シュニッツェル　★子牛などの肉のカツレツ　❸with the repugnance: 嫌悪感もあらわに　❹grandly sipped it all down: それ（牡蠣の汁）を堂々と飲み干した　❺was already half tipsy from drinking too fast: 飲むペースが速すぎて半分酔っていた ★tipsyは「ほろ酔いで」。　❻a euphoric, aching energy: 幸福感にみちた、胸が疼くほどの活力 ★euphoricは「幸福感にあふれた」、achingは「心の疼く」。　❼brimming: （飲み物）いっぱいになっている　❽was flushed: 顔が火照っていた　❾caught the reflection of her face in . . .: 〜の

120　PET MILK by Stuart Dybek

僕たちはレモンを絞ってかけ、ホースラディッシュをつけて、牡蠣を口のなかに滑り込ませた。それから殻をシャンペンですすぎ、塩っぱい、冷たい汁を飲んだ。隣のテーブルでカツレツを食べているでっぷり太ったカップルが、嫌悪感もあらわに僕らをじろじろ眺めた。中西部で人前で牡蠣を食べていると、よくそういう目で見られるのだ。僕たちは笑って、牡蠣の汁を飲み干した。飲むペースが速すぎて、僕はもうほろ酔い気分になっていた。体のなかに、幸福感にみちた、胸が疼くほどの活力がみなぎり出していた。ケイトがシャンペンのなみなみ入った牡蠣の殻を僕に向けて持ち上げ、「平和部隊に乾杯！」と言った。
　「ヨーロッパに乾杯！」と僕も応えて、僕たちは殻をかちんと鳴らした。
　ケイトは自分のワイングラスを僕のグラスに触れて、「誕生日おめでとう」と囁いた。そして、出し抜けにテーブルごしに身を乗り出し、僕にキスしてくれた。
　ふたたび腰を下ろすと、ケイトの頬は紅潮していた。テーブルの上の、ガラスの額に入った「プラハの街頭音楽師たち」に、彼女の顔が映って見えた。いつもなら僕は、ケイトが鏡や窓に映っているのを見るのが大好きだった。映し出された彼女の美しさは、何度見ても僕をはっとさせた。一度、面と向かってそう言ってみたら、その褒め言葉をさえぎるように、「それはあなたが、何に目を向けたらいいかを覚えたからよ」と彼女は言った。まるで僕が、偶然何か大きな秘密を発見したみたいな言い方だった。でもその晩、架空のプラハに幽霊のように浮かぶケイトの鏡像を見ていると、何だかまるで、彼女が消えてしまった未来を見せられたような気がした。僕にはわかっていた。僕にとってこれ以上美しい女の子にはもう絶対出会えないだろう、と。

中に彼女の顔が映っているのを見た　❿ fend off the compliment: その褒め言葉をさえぎる

🎧 117

We ❶killed the champagne and sat ❷twining fingers across the table. I was sweating. I could feel the warmth of her through her skirt under the table and I touched her leg. We still hadn't ordered dinner. I left money on the table and we ❸steered each other out a little unsteadily.

"Rudi will understand," I said.

The street was blindingly bright. A reddish sun ❹angled just above ❺the rims of the tallest buildings. I took my suit coat off and flipped it over my shoulder. We stopped in the doorway of a shoe store to kiss.

"Let's go somewhere," she said.

My roommate would already be home at my place, which was closer. Kate lived up north, in Evanston. It seemed a long way away.

🎧 118

We cut down a side street, past a fire station, to a small park, but its gate was locked. I ❻pressed close to her against the tall iron fence. We could smell the lilacs from a bush just inside the fence, and when I jumped for an overhanging branch my shirt sleeve hooked on a fence spike and tore, and ❼petals rained down on us as the ❽sprig sprang from my hand.

🎧 119

We walked to the subway. The evening rush was ❾winding down;

---

❶kill(ed) the champagne: シャンペンを飲み干す　❷twining fingers: 指をからませて　❸steered each other out: たがいに導きあうように店を出た　❹angled: 斜めに照っていた　❺the rims of . . .: 〜の縁　❻press(ed) close to . . .: 〜にぎゅっと寄っていく　❼petals rained down on us: 花弁が雨のように僕たちの頭に降ってきた　❽sprig: 若枝　❾wind(ing) down: 終わりに近づく

122　PET MILK by Stuart Dybek

僕らはシャンペンを飲み干し、テーブルごしに指をからませて座っていた。僕は汗をかいていた。テーブルの下で、彼女の体の温もりがスカートを通して伝わってきた。僕は彼女の脚に手を触れた。僕らはまだ食事を頼んでいなかった。僕はテーブルにお金を置いた。二人とも危なっかしい足取りで、たがいに導きあうように店を出た。
　「ルーディはわかってくれるよ」と僕は言った。
　街は目もくらむほどのまぶしさだった。赤っぽい太陽が、いちばん高いビルのすぐ上で斜めに照っていた。僕はスーツの上着を脱いで、肩に引っかけた。僕たちは靴屋の店先で立ちどまってキスをした。
　「どこかへ行きましょうよ」とケイトが言った。
　僕のアパートのほうが近かったけれど、僕のルームメートはもう帰ってきているだろう。彼女の住まいは北のエヴァンストン。それははてしなく遠いところに思えた。
　僕たちは近道をして裏通りを抜け、消防署の前を通って、小さな公園に着いた。でも門には鍵が掛かっていた。背の高い鉄柵の前で、僕は彼女を抱き寄せた。柵のすぐ向こうの茂みに生えたライラックの香りが漂ってきた。頭上に垂れている枝に飛びつこうと、僕は思いきりジャンプした。シャツの裾が、柵の尖った先に引っかかって破れてしまった。若枝が僕の手から弾け出て、花弁が雨のように僕たちの頭に降ってきた。
　僕たちは地下鉄の駅まで歩いていった。夕方のラッシュは終わりかけ

we must have caught the last express heading toward Evanston. Once the train climbed from the tunnel to the elevated tracks, it wouldn't stop until the end of the line, on Howard. There weren't any seats together, so we ❶stood swaying at the front of the car, beside the empty conductor's compartment. We ❷wedged inside, and I clicked the door shut.

🎧 120

The train ❸rocked and jounced, ❹clattering north. We were kissing, trying to catch the rhythm of the ride with our bodies. The sun bronzed the windows on our side of the train. I lifted her skirt over her knees, hiked it higher so the sun shone off her thighs, and ❺bunched it around her waist. She wouldn't stop kissing. She was moving her hips ❻to pin us to each jolt of the train.

🎧 121

We were speeding past scorched brick walls, gray windows, back porches outlined in sun, roofs, and treetops—the landscape of ❼the El I'd memorized from subway windows ❽over a lifetime of rides: ❾the podiatrist's foot sign past Fullerton; the bright pennants of Wrigley Field, at Addison; ancient hotels with ❿with TRANSIENTS WELCOME signs ⓫on their flaking back walls; ⓬peeling and graffiti-smudged billboards; the old cemetery just before Wilson Avenue. Even without looking, I knew almost exactly where we were. Within the compartment, the sound of our quick breathing was louder than the clatter of tracks. I was trying to slow down, to ⓭make it all

---

❶stood swaying: 揺られながら立っていた　❷wedged inside: 体を横にして狭い空間に身を押し入れた　❸rock(ed) and jounce(d): がたごとと弾むように揺れる　❹clatter(ing) north: 北へ向かってがたごと進む　❺bunch(ed) it around her waist: スカートを彼女の腰にたばねる　❻to pin us to each jolt of the train: 列車のごとん、ごとんという揺れに僕たちを貼りつけようと　❼the El: 高架鉄道　★=elevated railway　❽over a lifetime of rides: 一生涯ずっと乗ってきたなかで　❾the podiatrist's foot sign: 足の絵を描いた、足病専門医の看板　❿transients welcome:

ていた。僕らが乗ったのはたぶん、エヴァンストン方面に行く最後の快速列車だったのだろう。トンネルを出て高架線路に出ると、列車は終点のハワードまで止まらなかった。二人一緒に座れる席は空いていなかったので、僕たちは車両のいちばん前で、揺られながら立っていた。その横は空っぽの車掌室だった。僕らは体を横にして狭い空間に身を押し入れた。僕はドアをかしゃっと閉めた。

　北へ向かって疾走する列車は、がたごとと弾むように揺れた。僕たちはキスをしながら、体で列車のリズムをつかまえようとしていた。太陽が僕らの乗っている側の窓をブロンズ色に染めた。僕はケイトのスカートを膝の上まで持ち上げた。さらに高く引き上げると、太陽が彼女の太腿に当たって輝いた。僕はスカートを彼女の腰にたばねた。彼女はキスをやめなかった。腰をくねらせて、彼女は、列車のごとん、ごとんという揺れに僕たちを貼りつけようとしていた。

　列車は見るみる、焼け焦げた煉瓦の壁を過ぎ、灰色の窓を過ぎ、太陽と屋根と樹木に縁どられた裏庭を過ぎていった。僕にとっては、生まれてからずっと高架に乗りつづけて、隅から隅まで知りつくした風景だった。フラートンを越えたあたりの、足の絵を描いた、足病専門医の看板。アディソンの、リグリー球場にたなびく華やかなペナント。剝げかけた裏壁に「一夜泊り歓迎」と看板を出したおそろしく古いホテル。破れかけた落書きで汚れた広告板。ウィルソン・アベニューに出る直前の古い共同墓地。わざわざ見なくても、自分たちがいまどこにいるのか、手にとるようにわかった。車掌室のなかで、僕たちのせわしない息づかいは、線路の喧噪よりも大きく聞こえた。僕はスピードを緩めようとしていた。すべてをもっと長続きさせようとしていた。そして、彼女が手

短期滞在客歓迎　★かつては長期滞在者を主に対象とするホテルもあったため。　⓫on their flaking back walls: 剝げかけた裏壁に　⓬peeling and graffiti-smudged billboards: 剝がれかけた、落書きで汚れた広告板　⓭make it all last: そうしたすべてを（できるだけ長く）持続させる

last, and when she covered my mouth with her hand I turned my face to the window and looked out.

🎧 122

The train was braking a little from express speed, as it did each time it passed a local station. I could see blurred faces on the long wooden platform watching us pass—businessmen glancing up from folded newspapers, women ❶clutching purses and shopping bags. I could see the expression on each face, momentarily ❷arrested, as we flashed by. A high school kid ❸in shirt sleeves, maybe sixteen, with books tucked under one arm and a cigarette in his mouth, caught sight of us, and in the instant before he disappeared he grinned and started to wave. Then he was gone, and I turned from the window, back to Kate, forgetting everything—the passing stations, the glowing late sky, even the sense of missing her—but that ❹arrested wave stayed with me. It was as if I were standing on that platform, with my schoolbooks and a smoke, on one of those endlessly accumulated afternoons after school when I stood almost outside of time simply waiting for a train, and I thought how much I'd have loved seeing someone like us ❺streaming by.

---

❶clutching: 〜をしっかり抱えた　❷arrested: 注意を惹かれた　❸in shirt sleeves: ワイシャツ姿の　❹arrested: 停止したままの　❺stream(ing) by: 通過する

で僕の口を覆うと、僕は窓の方をふり返り、外を見た。

　列車は少し速度を落としていた。通過駅の前を過ぎるたびにそうするのだ。木造の細長いプラットホームの上のぼやけた顔たちが、僕らの列車が通過するのを眺めているのが見えた。折りたたんだ新聞からふと目を上げたサラリーマン、ハンドバッグや買物バッグをしっかり抱えた婦人たち。一つひとつの顔に浮かぶ表情も見えた。列車が目の前を飛ぶように過ぎる瞬間、一瞬それらの表情が静止する。たぶん十六歳くらいだろう、シャツの袖をまくり上げて小わきに教科書を抱え、口に煙草をくわえていた高校生が僕たちに気づき、その姿が見えなくなる直前に、にやっと笑って手を振りはじめた。次の瞬間、高校生はもう消えていた。僕は窓からケイトに目を戻し、何もかも忘れてしまった。通過駅も、夕焼け空も、彼女がいなくなって寂しいような気持ちさえも。でも、振りはじめたままぴたっと静止したその腕だけは忘れなかった。まるで、僕自身が教科書を抱え煙草をくわえてあのホームに立っているような気がした ── かつて、放課後の、はてしなく積み重ねられていった午後に、まるで時間の外に出てしまったみたいにぽつんと列車を待っていたときのように。そして僕は思うのだった。あのころ、僕らみたいなカップルが通過していくのが見られたらきっと素敵だったろうな、と。

Story 5
🎧 123-138

SNOWMEN
by
Steven Millhauser
雪人間
スティーヴン・ミルハウザー

　少年小説は、子供の視点から語られるのであれば、語彙も子供が使いそうな言葉に限定し、文章もシンプルにするのが「筋」だろうが、スティーヴン・ミルハウザーの文章は、そうした暗黙の掟を平然と無視する。雪の日にふだんと同じように朝食を食べさせられることに素直に驚く子供が語り手でありながら、その文章は端正にして緻密、語彙も豊か。語り手のなかに、子供と大人が混在しているのだ（もちろん、ミルハウザーの小説に出てくる子供はいつも、そうした「反則」がむしろ相応しいような、あらかじめ老成したような子供ではあるのだが）。
　子供たちの作る雪だるまが、わずか数日で西洋の美術史を一気に反復するかのような目まぐるしさでどんどん精緻になっていく。白一色に包まれた世界に魅せられた子供たちが、最終的には太陽と多色の世界に明るく戻っていくという展開も魅力的だが、まずは何といっても、雪人間一人ひとりの緻密な描写によって読み手を魅了する作品である。細部にあまりこだわらず「だいたい流れをつかむ」読み方も小説の場合大いに有効だと思うが、ことミルハウザーに関しては、徹底的に辞書を引いて、細部を味わうのが得策だと思う。

🎧 123

One sunny morning I woke and pushed aside a corner of the blinds. Above the frosted, sun-dazzled bottom of the glass I saw a brilliant blue sky, ❶divided into luminous rectangles by the orderly white strips of wood in my window. Down below, the back yard had vanished. In its place was a ❷dazzling white sea, whose ❸lifted and immobile waves ❹would surely have toppled if I had not looked at them just then. It had happened secretly, in the night. It had snowed ❺with such abandon, such fervor, such furious delight, that I could not understand how that wildness of snowing had failed to wake me with its white roar. The topmost twigs of ❻the tall backyard hedge poked through the whiteness, but here and there a great drift covered them. The silver chains of the bright-yellow swing-frame ❼plunged into snow. Snow rose high above the floor of the old chicken coop at the back of the garage, and snow on the chicken-coop roof ❽swept up to the top of the garage gable. In the corner of the white yard the tilted clothespole rose out of the snow like the mast of a sinking ship. ❾A reckless snow-wave, having dashed against the side of the pole, ❿flung up a line of frozen spray, as if straining to pull it all under. From the flat roof of the chicken coop ⓫hung a row of thick icicles, some in sun and some in shade. They reminded me of ⓬glossy and matte prints in my father's albums. Under the sunny icicles were dark holes in the snow where the water dripped. Suddenly I remembered a rusty rake-head

---

❶ divided into luminous rectangles: いくつものまばゆい長方形に分割されている　❷ dazzling: 目もくらむほどの、まぶしい　❸ lifted and immobile waves: こんもり盛り上がった、不動の波　❹ would surely have toppled: 間違いなく砕け落ちていただろう　❺ with such abandon, such fervor, such furious delight: 途方もなく奔放に、猛烈に、荒々しい歓喜とともに　❻ the tall backyard hedge: 裏庭の背の高い生け垣　❼ plunged into snow: ★直訳は「雪に飛び込んでいた」。　❽ swept up to . . .: 〜にまで広がっていた　❾ A reckless snow-wave: ★直訳は「向こう見ずな雪

ある晴れた朝に僕は目を覚まし、ブラインドの隅を押しのけてみた。霜のついた、まぶしく陽光を照り返すガラス窓から空を仰ぐと、抜けるように明るい青空が見えた。縦横に整然と並ぶ白い木の窓枠によって、空はいくつものまばゆい長方形に分割されている。下を見ると、裏庭が消えていた。代わってそこには目もくらむ真白い海があった。こんもり盛り上がった、不動の波をたたえている海。もしその瞬間に僕の視線がそれを捕えることがなかったら、波は間違いなく砕け落ちていただろう。すべては夜のあいだに、ひそかに起こったのだ。途方もなく奔放に、猛烈に、荒々しい歓喜とともに雪が降ったのだ。激しく降りしきる雪の白い怒号に、どうして僕は目を覚まさなかったのだろう？　裏庭の背の高い生け垣のてっぺんの小枝が、あたり一面を覆う白さの中から顔をのぞかせている。けれどそれらの小枝にしても、ところどころに吹きだまりの雪がかぶさっていた。明るい黄色のブランコ枠から吊り下がった銀色の鎖は、雪に埋もれて途中でとだえていた。ガレージの裏手にある古い鶏小屋の床にも雪はうず高く積もり、小屋の屋根の雪はガレージの切妻屋根のてっぺんにまで広がっていた。白い庭の片隅で、斜めにかしいだ物干し用の柱が、沈みゆく船のマストのように雪の中にそびえ立っている。まるでそれを引きずりおろそうとするかのように、雪の波は容赦なく柱に叩きつけ、凍りついたしぶきを投げ上げていた。鶏小屋の平べったい屋根から何本もの太いつららが、あるものは日なたに、あるものは日蔭に垂れ下がっている。それを見ていると、艶出しの写真と艶消しの写真が交互に並んだ父さんのアルバムを思い出した。陽を浴びたつららの下には水が垂れ、雪の表面に暗い穴ができている。僕はふ

の波」。　❿flung up: 〜を投げ上げていた　★flingは「〜を投げる」。　⓫hung a row of thick icicles: 何本もの太いつららが垂れ下がっていた　★倒置　⓬glossy and matte prints: 艶出しの写真と艶消しの写真

lying teeth down in the dirt of the vegetable garden. It seemed more completely buried than ships under the sea, or ❶the quartz and flint arrowheads that were said to lie under the dark loam of the garden, too far down for me to ever find them, forever out of reach.

🎧 124

I hurried downstairs, shocked to discover that I was expected to eat breakfast on such a morning. In the sunny yellow kitchen I dreamed of dark tunnels in the snow. There was no exit from the house that day except by way of the front door. A thin, dark, wetly gleaming trail led between high snowbanks to the two cement steps before the buried sidewalk, where it stopped abruptly, as if in sudden discouragement. Jagged hills of snow thrown up by the snowplow rose higher than my head. I climbed over ❷the broken slabs and reached ❸the freedom of the street. Joey Czukowski and Mario Salvio were already there. They seemed ❹struck with wonder. Earmuffs up and cap-peaks pulled low, they both held snowballs in their hands, as if they did not know what to do with them. Together we roamed the neighborhood in search of Jimmy Shaw. Here and there great gaps appeared in the snow-ranges, revealing a plowed driveway and a vista of snowy yard. At the side of Mario's house a sparkling drift swept up to the windowsill. A patch of bright-green grass, in a valley between drifts, startled us as if waves

---

❶ the quartz and flint arrowheads: 石英や火打ち石の矢じり　❷ the broken slabs: ★文字どおりには「割れた石板」。雪をそのようにたとえている。　❸ the freedom of the street: 自由あふれる街路　❹ struck with wonder: 驚異の念に打たれて

と、錆びついた熊手の刃が、先っぽを下に菜園の土の中に埋もれていることを思い出した。刃はいまや水底に沈んだ船よりも、菜園の薄黒い土壌の下に眠っているといわれる石英や火打ち石の矢じりよりも、完璧に埋もれてしまったように思えた。僕には決して見つからないくらい深い、永久に届かないところに。

　僕は急いで一階へ降りていった。こんな朝だというのに、いつも通り朝食の仕度ができているのを見て、僕はショックを覚えた。陽の当たる黄色い台所で、僕は雪の中の暗いトンネルを夢見た。今日は外に出るにも表玄関から出るしかない。黒っぽい、水気を含んで光る狭い小道が、両側に高く積まれた雪をしたがえて伸び、歩道に通じた二段のセメントの階段まで達している。そして雪に埋もれた歩道まで来ると、小道はあたかも急にやる気をなくしてしまったかのように、唐突にとだえていた。除雪車が投げ上げたぎざぎざの雪の丘は、僕の頭よりも高かった。僕は丘の崩れかけた部分を乗り越え、自由あふれる街路に出た。ジョーイ・ツコウスキーとマリオ・サルヴィーオが一足先にそこに来ていた。彼らは驚異の念に打たれているように見えた。耳覆いを引っぱり上げ、帽子のつばを押し下げて、両手に雪の玉を抱えている。二人ともまるで、それをどうしたらいいのかわからずにいるみたいだ。僕らは一緒に近所を歩きまわって、ジミー・ショーを探した。雪の山脈が並ぶ中、ところどころに大きな間隙があり、雪かきを終えた私道や、雪野原の広がる中庭が見えた。マリオの家の脇では、きらきら光る吹きだまりが窓枠の高さまで積もっていた。吹きだまりと吹きだまりのあいだで、明るい緑の芝生があたかも谷間のように顔をのぞかせて、僕らをはっと驚かせた。まるで海の底を眺めていて、突然波がぱっくり左右に分かれたみた

had parted and we were looking at the bottom of the sea. High above, white and black against the summer-blue sky, the telephone wires were heaped with snow. Heavy snow-lumps ❶fell thudding. We found Jimmy Shaw banging a stick against a snow-covered stop sign on Collins Street. Pagliaro's lot disturbed us: in summer we fought there with ashcan covers, sticks, and rusty cans, and now its dips and rises, its ripples and contours, which we knew as intimately as we knew our cellar floors, had been transformed into a mysterious new pattern of ❷humps and hollows, an unknown realm reminding us of the vanished lot only by the distorted swelling of its central hill.

🎧 125

Dizzy with discovery, we spent that morning wandering the newly invented streets of ❸more alien neighborhoods. From a roof gutter hung a glistening four-foot icicle, thick as a leg. Now and then we made snowballs, and ❹feebly threw ourselves into the conventional postures of a snowball fight, but our hearts were not really in it—they had surrendered utterly to the inventions of the snow. There was about our snow ❺a lavishness, an ardor, that made us restless, exhilarated, and a little uneasy, ❻as if we had somehow failed to measure up to that white extravagance.

🎧 126

It was not until the afternoon that the first snowmen appeared. There may have been some in the morning, but I did not see them,

---

❶ fell thudding: どさっ、どさっ、と落ちてきた　❷ humps and hollows: なだらかなこぶや窪み　❸ more alien neighborhoods: ふだんはあまり行かない一帯　❹ feebly threw ourselves into . . .: なんとなく〜に身を投じる　★feeblyは「弱々しく、力なく」。　❺ a lavishness, an ardor: ある種の豊潤さ、情熱のようなもの　❻ as if we had somehow failed to measure up to that white extravagance: まるで僕たちが、この白い贅沢にはふさわしくない卑小な存在であるかのように★ fail to measure up to . . . で「(期待など)にこたえ損ねる」。

いな感じだった。頭の上では、たっぷり雪をしょい込んだ電話線が、夏のように青い空を背景に、白と黒の線をくっきり浮かび上がらせている。大きな雪の固まりが、どさっ、どさっ、と音を立てて落ちてきた。
　僕らはコリンズ・ストリートでジミー・ショーを見つけた。ジミーは雪に覆われた止まれの標識を棒切れで叩いていた。パグリアーロの空地は僕たちを戸惑わせた。夏のあいだ、僕らはそこで、ゴミ入れの蓋や棒切れや錆びた缶カラを武器に戦争ごっこをしたものだった。あちこちの凹みや出っぱりも、さざ波のようにうねるその輪郭も、わが家の地下室の床のように僕らは慣れ親しんでいた。なのに今日は、その何もかもが不思議なかたちに変貌していた。なだらかなこぶや窪みが織りなす見たこともない空間。それは未知の領域だった。まん中の盛り上がった部分の、妙に歪んだ膨らみだけが、消えてしまった空地を思い出させる唯一の手がかりだった。
　発見に目もくらむ思いで、僕たちはその朝を、ふだんはあまり行かない一帯の、創造されたばかりの街並をさまよって過ごした。ある屋根の雨どいから、長さ一メートルを越える、人間の脚のように太いつららがきらきら光って垂れ下がっていた。僕らはときどき思い出したように雪玉を作り、ありきたりの雪合戦の真似事をしてみるのだったが、どうにも身が入らなかった。僕らの心は雪がつくり出したものたちにすっかり酔いしれていたのだ。僕らの町に降った雪には、ある種の豊潤さ、情熱のようなものがあって、それが僕たちを落着かなくし、僕たちの気持ちを高揚させ、そしていくらか不安にした。まるで僕たちが、この白い贅沢にはふさわしくない卑小な存在であるかのように。
　最初の雪人間たちが現われたのは、もう昼も過ぎた頃だった。午前中

or perhaps they were only the usual kind and remained ❶lost among the enchantments of the snow. But that afternoon we began to notice them, ❷in the shallower places of front and back yards. And we accepted them at once, indeed were soothed by them, as if only they could have been the offspring of such snow. They were not commonplace snowmen composed of three big snowballs piled one on top of the other, with carrots for noses and big black buttons or smooth round stones for eyes. No, they were passionately detailed men and women and children of snow, with noses and mouths and chins of snow. They wore hats of snow and coats of snow. Their shoes of snow were tied with snow-laces. One snowgirl in a summer dress of snow and a straw hat of snow stood holding a delicate snow-parasol over one shoulder.

🎧 127

I imagined that some child in the neighborhood, made restless by our snow, had fashioned the first of these snow statues, perhaps little more than an ordinary snowman ❸with roughly sculpted features. Once seen, the snowman had been swiftly imitated in one yard after another, always with some improvement—and in that rivalry that passes from yard to yard, ❹new intensities of effort had led to finer and finer figures. But perhaps I was mistaken. Perhaps the truth was that a child of genius, ❺maddened and inspired by our fervent snow, had ❻in a burst of rapture created a new kind of

---

❶lost among the enchantments of the snow: 雪の生んださまざまな魔法に埋もれてしまって ❷in the shallower places of front and back yards: ★直訳は「家々の前庭や裏庭の、比較的雪の浅い場所に」。 ❸with roughly sculpted features: ごく大雑把に目鼻を彫っただけの　★featureは目・鼻・口などの「顔の作り」。 ❹new intensities of effort: ★文字どおりには「新たな烈しさを伴った努力」。 ❺maddened and inspired by our fervent snow: 町に降った激しい雪に狂おしい霊感を受け★maddenは「〜を発狂させる」、inspireは「〜に霊感を与える」、ferventは「激しい」。

にもいくつか出ていたのかもしれないが、僕の目には入らなかった。あるいはそれらはごくありきたりの雪だるまにすぎず、雪の生んださまざまな魔法に囲まれてさっぱり目立たなかったのかもしれない。けれど午後になると、家々の庭の比較的雪の浅い場所に、僕らは雪人間たちの姿を認めはじめた。僕たちはすぐさま彼らの存在を受け入れた。彼らを見て気持ちが和みさえした。彼らだけが、これほどの雪の子孫たるにふさわしいように思えた。彼らはそんじょそこらにあるような、三段重ねの大きな雪玉、鼻は人参、目は大きな黒いボタンか滑らかな丸石といったたぐいの雪だるまとはわけが違っていた。そう、彼らは、細部に至るまで情熱を込めて作られた雪の男、雪の女、雪の子供だった。鼻も口も顎も、みんな雪だった。彼らは雪の帽子をかぶり、雪のコートを着ていた。雪の靴は雪の靴ひもでしばってあった。雪のサマードレスを着て、雪の麦わら帽子をかぶった一人の雪の女の子が、華奢なつくりの雪のパラソルを肩に載せて立っていた。

　僕は思った。きっとこのあたりの子供が、町に降った雪に心をかき乱されて、これら雪の彫像たちの第一号を作ったのだろう、と。おそらくそれは、ごく大雑把に目鼻を彫っただけの、ありきたりの雪だるまとさして変わらないものだったにちがいない。だがひとたびそれが人目にとまるや、またたく間にあちこちの庭で模倣され、新しい作品が作られるたびに何らかの改良が加えられていったのだ。そして、庭から庭へと競争が広がってゆくなか、注ぎ込まれる努力にも新たな真剣さが加わり、雪人間たちはますます洗練の度を増していったのだろう。だが実はそうではないかもしれない。こうも考えられる。つまりどこかの天才的な子供が、町に降った激しい雪に狂おしい霊感を受け、恍惚に酔いしれるま

❻ in a burst of rapture: 恍惚に酔いしれるまま

雪人間／スティーヴン・ミルハウザー

snowman, perfect in every detail, which others later copied ❶with varied success.

🎧 128

❷Fevered and summoned by those snowmen, we returned to our separate yards. I made my snowman in a hollow between the swing and the crab-apple tree. My first efforts were ❸clumsy and oppressive, but I ❹restrained my impatience and soon felt a passionate discipline come over me. My hands were inspired, it was as if I were coaxing into shape ❺a form that longed to spring forth from the fecund snow. I shaped the eyelids, gave a tenseness to the narrow nostrils, completed the tight yet faintly smiling lips, and stepped back to admire my work. Beyond the chicken coop, in Joey's yard, I saw him admiring his own. He had made an old woman ❻in a babushka, carrying a basket of eggs.

Together we went to Mario's yard, where we found him furiously completing the eyes of a caped and mustached magician who held in one hand a hollow top hat of snow from which he was removing a long-eared rabbit. We applauded him enviously and all three went off to find Jimmy Shaw, who had fashioned two small girls holding hands. I secretly judged his effort sentimental, yet was impressed by ❼his leap into doubleness.

🎧 129

❽Restless and unappeased, we set out again through the neighborhood, where already a change was evident. The ❾stiffly standing

---

❶with varied success: 直訳は「うまくいくこともあり、さほどでないこともあり」。　❷Fevered and summoned by . . .: 〜に熱中させられ、呼びよせられて　❸clumsy and oppressive: 不細工で気の滅入る　❹restrained my impatience: あせる気持ちを抑えた　❺a form that longed to spring forth from the fecund snow: 肥沃な雪の中から飛び出したくてうずうずしているもの　❻in a babushka: バブーシュカを巻いた　★babushkaは「(ロシアの農婦が使った)あごの下で結ぶ婦人用スカーフ」。　❼his leap into doubleness: 二人の人間を並べるという新機軸　❽Restless

ま、まったく新しい種類の、あらゆる細部に至るまで完璧な雪だるまを一つ創造し、それを見たほかの者たちが、不完全ではあれめいめい力の及ぶ限りに模倣したのかもしれないのである。
　雪人間たちにすっかり魅せられた僕らは、彼らに命令を受けたかのように、それぞれ自分の家の庭に戻っていった。僕はブランコとリンゴの木のあいだの窪みで自分の雪人間を作った。はじめのうちは不細工で気の滅入る出来映えだった。でもあせる気持ちを抑えて仕事を続けるうちに、ほどなく情熱的な集中力が自分を包むのを僕は感じた。僕の手は霊感を帯び、肥沃な雪の中から飛び出したくてうずうずしているものを優しく愛撫し、それにかたちを与えようと力を注いだ。僕は瞼を形づくり、狭い鼻孔に緊迫感を付与し、きっと結ばれた、しかしかすかに微笑んでいる唇を仕上げた。そして一歩退き、自分の作品にほれぼれと見入った。鶏小屋の向こうのジョーイの家の庭でも、ジョーイが同じように自作に見入っているのが見えた。彼の雪人間はバブーシカを巻いた老婆で、卵の入った籠を腕に抱えていた。
　僕たち二人がマリオの家へ行くと、マリオはちょうど、マントをまとい口髭を生やした手品師の目を懸命に仕上げている最中だった。手品師は片手に雪のシルクハットを持ち、その中から耳の長い兎を引っぱり出している。僕とジョーイは羨望の眼差しとともにマリオを賞讃し、それから三人でジミー・ショーを探しに行った。ジミーは手をつないだ二人の少女を完成したところだった。僕は心中ひそかにその作品の感傷癖を批判したけれど、二人の人間を並べるという新機軸には感心した。
　落着かない、満たされぬ思いを抱えて、僕たちはふたたび街へくり出した。街はすでに見逃しようもなく変化していた。午後も早い頃に見

and unappeased: 落着かない、満たされぬ思いで　❾ stiffly: ぎこちなく

雪人間／スティーヴン・ミルハウザー

snowmen we had seen earlier in the afternoon were giving way to snowmen that assumed a variety of poses. One, with head bent and a hand pressed to his hat, appeared to be walking into a wind, which blew back the skirt of his long coat. Another, ❶in full stride, had turned ❷with a frown to look over his shoulder, and you could see the ❸creases in his jacket of snow. A third bowed low from the waist, his hat swept out behind him. We returned dissatisfied to our yards. My snowman looked dull, stiff, and vague. I ❹threw myself into the fashioning of a more lively snowman, and as the sun sank below a rooftop I stood back to admire my snowy father, sitting in an armchair of snow with one leg hooked over the arm, holding a book in one hand as, with the other, he turned a single curling page of snow.

🎧 130

Yet even then I realized that it was not enough, that already it had been surpassed, that new forms yearned to be born from our restless, impetuous snow.

That night I could scarcely sleep. ❺With throbbing temples and burning eyes I hurried through breakfast and rushed outside. It was just as I had suspected: ❻a change had been wrought. I could feel it everywhere. Perhaps bands of feverish children, tormented by white dreams, had worked secretly through the night.

🎧 131

The snowmen had grown more marvelous. Groups of snowy fig-

---

❶in full stride: 大またで歩きながら　❷with a frown: 顔をしかめて　❸creases: 皺、折り目　❹threw myself into...: 奮起して〜した　❺With throbbing temples and burning eyes: ずきずき疼くこめかみと、燃えるように熱い目を抱えて　❻a change had been wrought: 大きな変化が生じていた　★wroughtはworkの過去・過去分詞の古い形。「作る」「引き起こす」の意味ではいまもよく使われる。

た、ぎこちなく立ちつくす雪人間たちに代わって、それぞれ独自のポーズをとった雪人間が主流になってきていた。ある男は頭を低く垂れ片手で帽子を押さえ、風に逆らって歩いていた。長いコートのすそが、風に吹かれて後ろになびいていた。またある者は、大またで歩きながら、顔をしかめて肩ごしに後ろをふり向いたところだった。雪の上着の皺までがはっきり見てとれた。さらにある者は、深々と御辞儀でもするみたいに体を二つに曲げていて、その帽子は後ろに吹きとばされてしまっている。僕らはしょげ返って自分の家の庭へ帰った。僕らの雪人間はぱっとしない、ぶざまな、ぼんやりとしたものに見えた。僕は奮起して、もっと生き生きした雪人間の製作に取りかかった。そして、太陽が屋根の下に沈む頃、一歩後ろに下がって、僕の雪の父さんを賞讃のまなざしで眺めた。雪の父さんは雪の肱掛け椅子に座って、片脚を肱掛けに載せ、一方の手に本を持ち、もう一方の手で丸まった雪の一ページをめくっていた。

　けれども僕はそのときすでに、これでもまだ十分とはいえないことに気づいていた。これよりももっと良いものがもう作られてしまっているのだ。僕たちの町に降った、せわしなく駆り立てられた雪から、さまざまな新しいかたちが生まれ出たいと焦がれているのだ。

　その晩、僕はほとんど眠れなかった。次の朝、ずきずき疼くこめかみと、燃えるように熱い目を抱えて、僕は大急ぎで朝食を済ませ、表に飛び出していった。思った通りだ。そこには大きな変化が生じていた。僕はその変化をいたるところに感じとることができた。おそらく熱にうなされるように白い夢に苛まれた子供たちが集まって、ひそかに夜通し黙々と働いたのだ。

　雪人間たちはいっそう見事になっていた。雪でできた人々の集いがそ

ures were everywhere. In one back yard I saw three ice skaters of snow, their heels lifted and their scarves of snow streaming out behind them. In another yard I saw, ❶gripping their instruments deftly, the fiercely playing members of a string quartet. Individual figures had grown more ❷audacious. On a back-yard clothesline I saw a snowy tightrope walker with a long balancing stick of snow, and in another yard I saw a ❸juggler holding two snowballs in one hand while, suspended in the air, directly above his ❹upward-gazing face. . . . But it was precisely a feature of that second day, when the art of the snowman appeared to ❺reach a fullness, that one could no longer be certain to what extent the act of seeing had itself become infected by these ❻fiery snow-dreams. And just when it seemed that nothing further could be dreamed, the snow animals began to appear. I saw a snow lion, a snow elephant with uplifted trunk, a snow horse rearing, a snow gazelle. But once ❼the idea of "snowman," already fertile with instances, had blossomed to include animals, new and ❽dizzying possibilities presented themselves, for there was suddenly nothing to prevent ❾further sproutings and germinations; and it was then that I began to notice, among the graceful white figures and ❿the daring, exquisite animals, ⓫the first maples and willows of snow.

🎧 132

It was on the afternoon of that second day that the passion for replication reached heights none of us could have foreseen. ⓬Sick

---

❶gripping their instruments deftly: しかるべく楽器を抱え　★deftlyは「器用に、巧みに」。
❷audacious: 大胆な　❸juggler: 投げ物芸人　❹upward-gazing: じっと頭上を凝視している
❺reach a fullness: 爛熟の域に達する　❻fiery snow-dreams: 狂おしい雪の夢の産物　❼the idea of "snowman," already fertile with instances:「雪人間」という観念が、すでにいくつもの実例ですっかり膨らんで　★fertileは「肥沃な、豊穣な」。　❽dizzying: 目もくらむような　❾further sproutings and germinations: さらなる成長といっそうの発芽　❿the daring, exquisite

142　SNOWMEN by Steven Millhauser

こら中に出現していた。ある家の裏庭では、三人の雪人間がアイス・スケートをしていた。彼らのかかとは宙に浮き、雪のスカーフが後ろになびいている。またある家の庭には、各自がしかるべく楽器を抱え、一心不乱に演奏している最中の弦楽四重奏団がいた。単独の人間たちもより大胆になっていた。ある家の裏庭の物干しロープの上に、長い雪のバランス棒を抱えた雪の綱渡り芸人がいた。別の家の庭にも玉投げをしている大道芸人がいて、片手に二個の雪玉を抱え、じっと頭上に注がれたその凝視の先にも、空中にぽっかりと……だがこれこそが二日目の特徴だった。雪人間作りの技術がどうやら爛熟の域に達したこの日、これら狂おしい雪の夢の産物に、見るという行為そのものがどこまで感染してしまったのか、もはやよくわからなくなってしまったのだ。そして、もうこれ以上のものを夢見ることなどありえないと思えてきたとき、雪動物たちが現われた。僕は雪ライオンを見た。鼻を持ち上げた雪象を見た。後ろ足で立っている雪馬、雪カモシカを見た。「雪人間」という、すでにすっかり膨らんだ発想が、ひとたび動物をも含むようになるやいなや、新たな、目もくらむようなさまざまな可能性が見えてきた。さらなる成長、いっそうの発芽を妨げるものが、突如何もなくなったのだ。そしてそのとき僕は、優雅な白い人々や、大胆で精妙な動物たちに混じって、最初の雪カエデと雪ヤナギの姿を認めたのだった。

　その二日目の午後、複製への情熱は、誰一人予想しえなかったほどの高みに達した。恍惚に心も朦朧となり、驚嘆の念にほとんど痛みを感じ

---

animals: 大胆で精妙な動物たち　❶ the first maples and willows of snow: 最初の雪カエデと雪ヤナギ　❷ Sick with ecstasy, pained with wonder: 恍惚に心も朦朧となり、驚嘆の念に痛みを感じながら

with ecstasy, pained with wonder, I walked the white streets with Joey Czukowski and Mario Salvio and Jimmy Shaw. "Look at that!" one of us would cry, and "❶Cripes, look at that!" Our own efforts had already been ❷left far behind, but it no longer mattered, for the town itself had been ❸struck with genius. Trees of snow had been composed leaf by leaf, with visible veins, and ❹upon the intricate twigs and branches of snow, ❺among the white foliage, one could see white sparrows, white cardinals, white jays. In one yard we saw a garden of snow tulips, row on row. In another yard we saw a snow fountain with arching water jets of ❻finespun snow. And in one back yard we saw an entire parlor all of snow, with snow lamps and snow tables and, in a snow fireplace, logs and flames of snow. Perhaps it was this display that inspired one of the more remarkable creations of that afternoon—in the field down by the stream, ❼dozens of furiously intense children were completing a great house of snow, with ❽turrets and gables and chimneys of snow, and splendid rooms of snow, with floors of snow and furniture of snow, and stairways of snow and mirrors of snow, and cups and rafters and sugar bowls of snow, and, on a mantelpiece of marble snow, a clock of snow with a moving ice ❾pendulum.

🎧 133

I think it was the very thoroughness of these successes that produced in me the first stirrings of uneasiness, for I sensed in our extravagant triumphs an inner impatience. Already, it seemed to me,

---

❶cripes: こりゃ参った ★やや古い感じのする語。 ❷left far behind: すっかり取り残されて ❸struck with genius: 天才の霊感に打たれて ❹upon the intricate twigs and branches of snow: その精緻（intricate）な雪の枝々には ★twigは「小枝、細枝」、branchは太さにかかわらず「枝」全般を指す。 ❺among the white foliage: 白く茂った葉のあいだに（隠れるようにして） ★foliageは「(1本の草木の) 葉 (全部)」。 ❻finespun: 糸のように細い ❼dozens of furiously intense children: 一心に働く何十人もの子供たち ❽turrets and gables and chimneys of

ながら、僕はジョーイ・ツコウスキーとマリオ・サルヴィーオとジミー・ショーと一緒に白い街並を歩いた。「見ろよ、あれ」と僕らの一人が叫ぶのだった。「すごいぞ、ほら、あれ！」。僕ら自身の作ったものはもうすっかり時代遅れになってしまっていた。でもそんなことはどうでもよかった。なぜならいまや町全体が天才の霊感に貫かれていたからだ。葉っぱ一枚一枚の葉脈まではっきり見える雪の木があちこちに立っていた。その精緻な雪の枝々には、白く茂った葉のあいだに隠れるようにして、白いスズメや白いコウカンチョウや白いカケスの姿が見えた。ある庭では雪のチューリップが花壇いっぱい、何列も何列も並んでいた。別の庭では、雪の噴水から吹き上げる、糸のように細い雪の水が空中に弧を描いていた。そしてまたある裏庭には、何から何まで雪でできた居間がそっくり一部屋作られていた。雪のランプに雪のテーブル、雪の暖炉には雪の薪と雪の炎。おそらくこの作品に刺激されて、この午後の傑作の一つが生まれたのだろう —— 川ぞいの野原で、一心に働く何十人もの子供たちが、大きな雪の邸宅をつくり上げていたのだ。雪の小塔、破風、煙突、いくつもの華麗な雪の部屋、床も家具も雪、階段も鏡も雪、茶碗も梁も砂糖壺も雪、そして雪の大理石のマントルピースの上には、左右に揺れる氷の振子のついた雪の置時計があった。

　これらの傑作の、あまりに徹底した完璧さが、おそらく僕の中にかすかな不安を生み出したのだろう。常軌を逸した力業の中に、僕は内なる焦燥を感じた。新しい雪人間たちを見ていると、その技術はもはや過剰

---

snow: 雪の小塔（turrets）、破風（gables）、煙突（chimneys）　❾pendulum: 振子

our snowmen were showing evidence of a skill so excessive, an elaboration so painfully and ❶exquisitely minute, that it could scarcely conceal a desperate restlessness. Someone had fashioned a leafy hedge of snow in which he had devised an intricate snow spiderweb, whose frail threads ❷shimmered in the late afternoon light. Someone else had fashioned a kaleidoscope of snow, which turned to reveal, in delicate ice mirrors, changing arabesques of snow. And on the far side of town we discovered an entire park of snow, already abandoned by its makers: the pine trees had pinecones of snow and individual snow needles, on the snow picnic tables lay fallen acorns of snow, snow burrs caught on our trouser legs, and under an abandoned swing of snow I found, beside an empty Coke bottle made of snow, a snow nickel ❸with a perfectly rendered buffalo.

🎧 134

Exhausted by these ❹prodigies, I ❺sought to pierce the outward shapes and seize the unquiet essence of the snow, but I saw only whiteness there. That night I spent in anxious dreams, and I woke feverish and unrefreshed to a sunny morning.

🎧 135

The world was still white, but snow was dripping everywhere. Icicles, longer and more lovely, shone forth in a last, desperate brilliance, rainspouts trickled, ❻rills of bright black snow-water rushed along the sides of streets and poured through ❼the sewer grates. I

---

❶exquisitely minute: この上なく（exquisitely）精密な（minute）　★この意味でのminuteの発音は[mainjúːt]。　❷shimmer(ed): ちらちらと光る　❸with a perfectly rendered buffalo: 野牛の姿が完璧に彫り込まれた（rendered）　★1913-38に鋳造された五セント貨の模様。　❹prodigies: 離れ業、驚異　❺sought to pierce the outward shapes: 表面のかたちの奥を見通そうとした　❻rills of bright black snow-water: 明るい黒の雪どけ水が集まってできた小川（rills）　❼the sewer grates: 下水道（sewer）の格子（grates）

の域に達しているように思えた。それを作るために注ぎ込まれたこの上ない細心さと入念さを思うと、ほとんど痛ましさを感じずにはいられなかった。その奥にひそむ、追い立てられるような苛立ちは隠しようもなかった。ある者は葉のふさふさ茂った雪の生け垣を作ったが、そこには入り組んだ雪の蜘蛛の巣が張っていて、か細い糸が午後遅くの陽光を浴びてちらちらと光っていた。またある者は雪の万華鏡を作った。それを回すと、華奢な氷の鏡の上に、さまざまにかたちを変える雪のアラベスクが映し出された。そして町の向こう側に、雪の公園が一つまるごと、作り主たちにはすでに見捨てられて残っているのを僕らは発見した。松の木には雪の松ぼっくりがあり、雪の松葉も一本一本ついている。雪のピクニックテーブルの上には雪のどんぐりが落ちているし、雪のいがが僕らのズボンにくっついた。そして、見捨てられた雪のブランコの下で、雪でできたコーラの空瓶のかたわらに、野牛の姿が完璧に彫り込まれた雪の五セント貨が横たわっているのを僕は見つけた。

　これらの離れ業に疲れはてた僕は、表面のかたちの向こうに、雪の持つその落着かない本質を見据えようとした。だがそこに見えるのは白さばかりだった。僕は不安な夢を見ながらその晩を過ごした。熱っぽく、疲れもとれぬまま目を覚ますと、外は晴れた朝だった。

　世界は相変わらず白かった。だが雪はいたるところでぽとぽとと垂れていた。つららは昨日よりも長く、美しく、最後の絶望的な輝きを発していた。雨どいから水がしたたり落ち、明るい黒の雪どけ水が小川となって道の両側を勢いよく流れ、下水道の格子の中に注ぎ込んだ。僕は

did not notice them at first, ❶the harbingers of the new order. It was Mario who pointed the first one out to me. From the corner of a roof it ❷thrust out over the rainspout. I did not understand it, but I was filled with happiness. I began to see others. They ❸projected from roof corners, high above the yards, their smiles ❹twisted in mockery. These gargoyles of snow had perhaps been shaped as a ❺whim, a joke, a piece of ❻childish exuberance, but as they spread through the town I began to sense their true meaning. They were nothing less than a protest against ❼the solemnity, the rigidity, of our snowmen. What had seemed a blossoming forth of hidden powers, that second afternoon, suddenly seemed ❽a form of intricate constriction. It was as if those bird-filled maples, those lions, those leaping ballerinas and ❾prancing clowns had been nothing but a failure of imagination.

🎧 136

On that third and last day, when our snowmen, ❿weary with consumption, ⓫swerved restlessly away, I sensed a fever in the wintry air, as if everyone knew that such strains and ecstasies were bound to end quickly. Scarcely had the gargoyles sprouted from the roofs when, among the trees and tigers, one began to see ⓬trolls and ogres and elves. They ⓭squatted in the branches of real elms and snow elms, they ⓮peeked out through ⓯the crossed slats of porch aprons, they hid behind the skirts of snow women. Fantastical snowbirds appeared, nobly lifting their white, impossible wings.

---

❶ the harbingers of the new order: 新たなる秩序の到来を告げる者たち　★harbingerは「先触れ、前兆」。　❷ thrust out over . . .: 〜の上につき出る　❸ projected: つき出した　❹ twisted in mockery: あざけるように歪んでいた　❺ whim: 気まぐれ　❻ childish exuberance: 子供っぽくはしゃいだ気持ち　★exuberanceは「幸福な気持ちや興奮が満ちた様」。　❼ the solemnity, the rigidity: 物々しさ、硬直ぶり　❽ a form of intricate constriction: 込み入った (intricate) 束縛 (constriction) の一形態　❾ prancing clowns: はね回る道化師たち　❿ weary with consumption:

はじめ、新たなる秩序の到来を告げる者たちに気がつかなかった。その第一号の存在を指摘してくれたのはマリオだった。ある家の屋根の角から、それは雨どいの上につき出ていた。なぜだかはよくわからなかったけれど、僕は幸福感でいっぱいになった。見ればあちこちに同じ姿が見える。家々の屋根の片隅からその身をつき出し、庭を見下ろす彼らの笑みは、あざけるように歪んでいた。これら雪の怪獣(ガーゴイル)たちは、もとはおそらくほんの気まぐれ、冗談として作られたものにちがいない。単に子供っぽくはしゃいだ気持ちの産物にすぎなかったのだろう。けれど、それが町じゅうに広がってゆくにつれて、僕にはその真の意味がだんだんと見えてきた。彼らは抗議にほかならないのだ。雪人間の厳粛さと硬直性に対する抗議なのだ。あの二日目の午後には隠れた能力の開花と見えたものが、いまや突如として、込み入った束縛の一形態になってしまったのである。無数の鳥がとまっているカエデの木、あのライオンたち、跳躍するバレリーナたち、はね回る道化師たち —— それらすべてが、単なる創造力の欠如の産物にすぎないように思えてきたのだ。

　その三日目の、最後の日、完全さに疲れはてた雪人間たちは、落着かなげに身をよじらせていた。冬の空気の中に、僕はある種の熱っぽさを感じた。それはあたかも、これほどの緊張、これほどの恍惚がじき終わるほかないことを、誰もが承知しているかのようだった。屋根の上から怪獣(ガーゴイル)たちが顔を出しはじめてからまもなく、木々や虎たちに混じって、小人や食人鬼や妖精たちが目につくようになった。彼らは本物の楡の木や雪の楡の木の枝に座り込み、玄関の雨よけの板ばり格子の陰から顔を出し、雪の女性たちのスカートの後ろに身を隠した。幻想の雪鳥たちが出現し、その白い、ありえない翼を気高くはばたかせた。半鷲半獅(グリフィン)、一

完全さ(consummation)に疲れはてて　⓫swerved restlessly away: 落着かなげにそれていった　⓬trolls and ogres and elves: 小人や食人鬼や妖精たち　⓭squat(ted): 座り込む　⓮peek(ed) out through . . .: から顔を出す　⓯the crossed slats of porch aprons: 玄関の雨よけの板ばり格子

❶Griffins, unicorns, and sea serpents enjoyed a brief reign before being surpassed by ❷splendid new creatures that disturbed us like half-forgotten dreams. Here and there rose ❸fanciful dwellings, like feverish castles, like fairy palaces glimpsed at the bottoms of lakes on vanished summer afternoons, with soaring pinnacles, twisting passageways, stairways leading nowhere, snow chambers seen in fever-dreams.

🎧 137

Yet even these visions of the morning ❹partook of the very world they longed to ❺supplant, and it was not until the afternoon that our snowmen began to achieve freedoms so dangerous that they threatened to burn out the eyes of ❻beholders. It was then that ❼distorted, elongated, disturbingly supple figures began to replace our ❽punctilious imitations. And yet I sensed that they were not distortions, ❾those ungraspable figures, but direct expressions of shadowy inner realms. To behold them was to be filled with a sharp, troubled joy. As the afternoon advanced, and the too-soon-darkening sky warned us of ❿transitory pleasures, I felt a last, intense straining. My nerves trembled, my ears rang with white music. A new mystery was visible everywhere. It was as if snow were throwing off ⓫the accident of accumulated heaviness and returning to its original airiness. Indeed these spiritual forms, ⓬disdaining the earth, seemed scarcely to be composed of white substance, as if they were striving to escape from the limits of snow

---

❶Griffins, unicorns, and sea serpents: 半鷲半獅・一角獣・大海蛇〔グリフィン〕　❷splendid new creatures: 新しい華麗な生き物たち　❸fanciful dwellings: 幻想の住居　❹partook of . . . : 〜の名残りがまだいくぶん残っていた　★partake of . . . は「〜の気味がある」。　❺supplant: 〜を駆逐する、〜に取って代わる　❻beholders: 見る者たち　❼distorted, elongated, disturbingly supple figures: 歪んだかたちの、妙に細長い、胸騒ぎのするほどしなやかな姿たち　❽punctilious imitations: 堅苦しい模倣　❾those ungraspable figures: しかとは捉えがたいそれらのかたち　❿transitory

角獣、大海蛇が王座を享受したのもつかの間、なかば忘れてしまった夢のように僕たちの心をかき乱す新しい華麗な生き物たちがそれに取って代わった。あちこちに幻想の住居が出現した。熱病にうなされる城郭のように、あるいは消えてしまった夏の午後に湖の底に垣間見たおとぎの宮殿のように、尖塔が空高くそびえ、くねくねと折れ曲がった通路があり、どこにもたどり着かない階段があり、熱病の夢で見る雪の寝室があった。

けれども、これら朝の幻想たちには、彼らが駆逐せんとしているこの現実界の名残りがまだいくぶん残っていた。その日の午後になって初めて、雪人間たちは、見る者の目を焼き焦がしかねないほどの危険な自由を獲得するようになった。歪んだかたちの、妙に細長い、胸騒ぎのするほどしなやかな姿たちが、それまでの几帳面な模倣を凌駕しはじめた。だが僕にはわかっていた。彼らは歪みなんかではない。しかとは捉えがたいそれらのかたちは、心の奥にひそむ影の世界をじかに表わしているのだ。それらを見ることは、刺すような悩ましい悦びに満たされることだった。夕暮れが迫り、あまりに早く暮れゆく空が僕たちに悦びのはかなさを警告するなか、僕は最後の、強烈な緊張を感じた。僕の神経はうち震え、耳では白い音楽が鳴っていた。新たなる神秘がいたるところにその姿を現わしていた。それはあたかも雪が、たまたま蓄積された重さをふり捨てて、本来の軽やかさに戻っていこうとしているかのようだった。地上を蔑むこれら霊的なかたちは、およそ白い物質から構成されているようには見えなかった。まるで雪それ自体の限界から逃れようと力

---

pleasures: はかない悦び　⓫ the accident of accumulated heaviness: たまたま蓄積された重さ　★直訳は「蓄積された重さという偶然」。　⓬ disdain(ing) the earth: 地上を蔑む

itself. Walking ❶the ringing streets in the last light, ❷my nerves stretched taut, I felt in that last ❸rapture of snow a lofty and criminal striving, and all my senses seemed to dissolve in ❹the dark pleasures of transgression.

🎧 138

❺Drained by these difficult joys, I was not unhappy when the rain came.

It rained all that night, and far into the morning. In the afternoon the sun came out. Bright-green grass shone among thin patches of snow. Joey Czukowski, Mario Salvio, Jimmy Shaw, and I roamed the neighborhood before returning to my cellar for a game of ping-pong. Brilliant black puddles shone in the sunny streets. Here and there on snow-patched lawns we saw remains of snowmen, but so melted and disfigured that they were only great lumps of snow. We did not discuss the events of the last few days, which already seemed as fantastic as vanished icicles, as unseizable as fading dreams. "Look at that!" cried Mario, and pointed up. On a telephone wire black as licorice, stretched against the bright blue sky, a bluejay sat and squawked. Suddenly it flew away. A dark-yellow willow burned in the sun. On a wooden porch step I saw a brilliant red bowl. "Let's do something," said Joey, and we tramped back to my house, our boots ❻scraping against the asphalt, our boot buckles ❼jangling.

---

❶ the ringing streets: 余韻を響かせる街　❷ my nerves stretched taut: 神経をぴんと張りつめて　❸ rapture: 歓喜　❹ the dark pleasures of transgression: 掟を破ることの暗い快楽　❺ Drained by these difficult joys: 狂おしい悦びにすっかり生気を吸い取られて　❻ scraping against . . .: 〜にこするようにして　❼ jangling: がちゃがちゃいわせて

の限りを尽くしているみたいだった。一日の最後の光を浴びて余韻を響かせる街なかを、張りつめた気持ちで歩きながら、僕は雪の最後の歓喜の中に、気高い、そして罪深い渇望を感じた。掟を破ることの暗い快楽に、僕の五感全部が溶けていく思いだった。

　狂おしい悦びにすっかり生気を奪われた僕は、雨が降り出したとき、内心ほっとしたくらいだった。

　雨はその夜一晩じゅう降りつづけ、翌朝になってもなかなか止まなかった。午後になって太陽が出てきた。明るい緑の芝生が薄い雪のパッチのあいだから鮮やかに輝いた。ジョーイ・ツコウスキー、マリオ・サルヴィーオ、ジミー・ショー、そして僕は、卓球をしに僕の家の地下室へ戻る道すがら、近所をぶらついてみた。明るい黒の水たまりが、陽に照らされた街路のあちこちで光っていた。雪がまだらに残った芝生の庭に、雪人間たちの残骸がいくつか目についた。彼らはすっかり溶けて変形してしまっていて、いまやただの大きな雪のかたまりにすぎなかった。僕たちは昨日までの三日間の出来事を話しあったりはしなかった。それらはもういまでは、溶けてしまったつららのようにはかなく、消えゆく夢のように捉えがたいものに思えた。「見ろよ、あれ！」とマリオが叫んで、上空を指さした。明るい青空を背景にぴんと伸びた、甘草飴のように真黒な電話線の上に、アオカケスが一羽とまってきいきい鳴いていた。突如それは飛び去った。くすんだ黄色の柳の木が一本、陽の光を一身に浴びていた。どこかの家の玄関の木の階段に、鮮やかな赤のボウルが一つ置かれていた。「何かして遊ぼうぜ」とジョーイが言った。僕たちはブーツをアスファルトにごしごしこするようにして、ブーツの止め金をがちゃがちゃいわせながら、僕の家へ戻っていった。

Story 6
🎧 139-164

AUGGIE WREN'S CHRISTMAS STORY
by
Paul Auster

オーギー・レンのクリスマス・ストーリー
ポール・オースター

　いわゆる「全知の語り手」が「あるところにおじいさんとおばあさんがいました」と言ったなら、我々は、「本当にあるところにおじいさんとおばあさんがいたのだろうか？」と問いはしない。が、誰か特定の人物が語り手である場合、我々はその人物が言うことをつねに疑ってかかる必要がある。カズオ・イシグロの『日の名残り』の語り手スティーヴンスのように、その裏の意味を読み手がつねに読むことになるような語り手を「信頼できない語り手」(unreliable narrator) と呼ぶが、原理的には、一人称の語り手はすべて「信頼できない語り手」である。
　この小説の後半で「掛け値なしの真実」と称する自分の体験談を語るオーギーも、実はそういう典型的「信頼できない語り手」の一バリエーションかもしれない。それに、そもそも、作者オースター自身を思わせる、クリスマスの日に載せる小説をニューヨーク・タイムズに依頼されてなかなか書けずにいる作家、という設定の語り手だって、やはり怪しい。何しろこの作品、元来、本当にニューヨーク・タイムズ1990年のクリスマス当日に掲載されたのだから (もちろん、そういう仕掛けが楽しく思えるかどうかは、まずはそれぞれの語り手が語る物語が面白いか否かにかかっているのだが)。
　映画『スモーク』では、後半のオーギーの物語を、オーギーを演じるハーヴェイ・カイテルが語っている。聞き較べてみるのも一興か。

🎧 139

 I heard this story from Auggie Wren. Since Auggie ❶doesn't come off too well in it, at least not as well as he'd like to, he's asked me not to use his real name. Other than that, ❷the whole business about the lost wallet and the blind woman and the Christmas dinner ❸is just as he told it to me.

 Auggie and I have known each other for close to eleven years now. He works behind the counter of a cigar store on Court Street in downtown ❹Brooklyn, and since it's the only store that carries the little Dutch cigars I like to smoke, I go in there fairly often. For a long time, I didn't give much thought to Auggie Wren. He was the strange little man who wore a hooded blue sweatshirt and sold me cigars and magazines, ❺the impish, wisecracking character who always had something funny to say about the weather or ❻the Mets or the politicians in Washington, and ❼that was the extent of it.

🎧 140

 But then one day several years ago he happened to be looking through a magazine in the store, and he ❽stumbled across a review of one of my books. He knew it was me because a photograph accompanied the review, and after that things changed between us. I was no longer ❾just another customer to Auggie, I had become a distinguished person. Most people ❿couldn't care less about books and writers, but it turned out that Auggie considered himself an artist. Now that he had ⓫cracked the secret of who I was, he ⓬em-

---

❶ doesn't come off too well: あまりいい役柄で出てくるわけではない　❷ the whole business about…: 〜についての何もかもが　❸ is just as he told it to me: 彼が私に物語ったままである　❹ Brooklyn: ★ニューヨークの一地域であるブルックリンには高級住宅地もあればスラムもあるが、このあたりはまず平均的な下町という感じ。　❺ the impish, wisecracking character: 茶目っ気のある (impish)、何かと気のきいたことを言う (wisecracking) 人物　❻ the Mets: ★ニューヨーカーにとって、球団メッツの動向は重大事。　❼ that was the extent of it: その程度のことだった

私はこの話をオーギー・レンから聞いた。オーギーはこの話のなかで、あまりいい役を演じていない。少なくとも、オーギー本人にとって願ってもない役柄とは言いがたい。そんなわけでオーギーからは、俺の本名は出さないでくれよな、と頼まれている。それをべつにすれば、落ちていた財布のことも、盲目の女性のことも、クリスマス・ディナーのことも、すべて彼が私に話してくれたとおりである。

　私がオーギーと知りあって、かれこれ十一年近くになる。彼の仕事場はブルックリンの繁華街、コート・ストリートにある葉巻店のカウンターである。私が好んで喫っている小さなオランダ葉巻を置いているのはこの店一軒なので、いきおいここには足しげく通うことになる。はじめの何年かは私も、オーギー・レンのことを特に気にとめていたわけではない。彼はフードつきの青いトレーナーを着た風変わりな小男であり、私に葉巻と雑誌を売ってくれる人物である。天気やメッツやワシントンの政治家連中をネタに何かと気のきいたことを言う、頭の回転の速い、茶目っ気のある男である。それだけのことだった。

　ところが、何年か前のある日、オーギーが店の雑誌をぱらぱらめくっていたときのこと、私の本の書評がたまたま彼の目にとまった。それが私だとわかったのは、書評には私の写真も添えてあったからである。それ以来、私たちの関係は一変した。オーギーにとって、私はもはや単なるその他大勢の客ではなかった。私は一人の名士になったのである。たいていの人は、本だの作家だのと聞いても、そんなもの犬も喰うかという顔しかしない。でもオーギーは違っていた。というのも、彼は自分を芸術家とみなしていたのだ。私の正体が解明されたいま、彼は私を同胞

---

❽ stumbled across a review of one of my books: たまたま私の本の書評を目にとめた　❾ just another customer: 単なる大勢の客の一人　❿ couldn't care less: どうでもいいと思っている　★決まり文句。　⓫ cracked: 〜を解決した　★=solved　⓬ embraced me as an ally: 私を同胞として熱く迎え入れた

braced me as an ally, a ❶confidant, a ❷brother-in-arms. To tell the truth, I found it rather embarrassing. Then, almost inevitably, a moment came when he asked me if I would be willing to look at his photographs. ❸Given his enthusiasm and goodwill, there didn't seem to be any way I could ❹turn him down.

🎧 141

❺God knows what I was expecting. ❻At the very least, it wasn't what Auggie showed me the next day. In a small, windowless room at the back of the store, he opened a cardboard box and pulled out twelve ❼identical black photo albums. This was his life's work, he said, and it didn't take him more than five minutes a day to do it. Every morning for the past twelve years, he had stood at the corner of Atlantic Avenue and Clinton Street at precisely seven o'clock and had taken a single color photograph of precisely the same view. The project now ran to more than four thousand photographs. Each album represented a different year, and all the pictures ❽were laid out in sequence, from January 1 to December 31, with the dates carefully recorded under each one.

🎧 142

As I ❾flipped through the albums and began to study Auggie's work, I didn't know what to think. My first impression was that it was the oddest, most bewildering thing I had ever seen. All the pictures were the same. The whole project was ❿a numbing onslaught of repetition, the same street and the same buildings over and over

---

❶confidant:（秘密などを打ち明けられる）親友　❷brother-in-arms: 戦友　★armsは武器、軍事などの意。　❸Given his enthusiasm and goodwill: 相手の熱心さと悪気のなさを思えば　❹turn him down: 断る、はねつける　❺God knows: 誰にもわからない＝自分でもわからない　❻At the very least: はっきり言えるのは、控えめに言っても　❼identical: たがいにまったく同じの　★sameより意味が強い。　❽were laid out in sequence: 順番に並べられていた　❾flipped through the albums: アルバムをぱらぱらめくっていった　❿a numbing onslaught of

として迎え入れた。親密な話し相手として、戦友として。正直言って、私としてはいささかありがた迷惑な話だと思った。やがて、やっぱり来たかという感じで、俺の写真を見てみないか、とオーギーが持ちかけてきた。見せたくてうずうずしている様子だし、むろん悪気もない。どうにも断われそうになかった。

　どんなものを見せられることになると思っていたのか、自分でもよくわからない。はっきり言えるのは、とにかく翌日オーギーが見せてくれたようなものは予想していなかったということだ。店の奥の、窓もない狭い部屋でダンボール箱を開けた彼は、みな同じ外見の黒いアルバムを十二冊取り出した。これが俺のライフワークなんだよ、と彼は言った。一日に五分とかからないけどね。過去十二年間、彼は毎朝欠かさず、七時きっかりにアトランティック・アベニューとクリントン・ストリートの交差点に立ち、まったく同じ場所を一枚ずつカラー写真に撮りつづけてきたのである。いまやその作品は四千枚以上に達していた。アルバム一冊にそれぞれ一年分の仕事が収められ、一月一日から十二月三十一日までの写真がきちんと順番に並んで、その一枚一枚の下に、几帳面な字で日付が書き込んであった。

　私はそれらのアルバムをぱらぱらとめくって、オーギーの作品をしげしげと眺めた。どう考えるべきなのか、私にはまるでわからなかった。私の第一印象は、こんなに奇妙な、こんなに訳のわからない代物を見たのは初めてだ、という思いだった。何しろ、どの写真も同じなのだ。作品全体が、これでもか、これでもかと迫ってくる、目もくらむほどの反復にほかならなかった。同じ道路、同じ建物が、何度も何度も出てく

---

repetition: ★直訳すれば「麻痺させるような反復の猛襲」。一見同じ写真が、これでもか、これでもか、と迫ってくるので感覚が麻痺してしまいそうだということ。

again, ❶an unrelenting delirium of redundant images. I couldn't think of anything to say to Auggie, so I continued turning pages, nodding my head ❷in feigned appreciation. Auggie himself ❸seemed unperturbed, watching me with ❹a broad smile on his face, but after I'd been at it for several minutes, he suddenly interrupted me and said, "You're going too fast. ❺You'll never get it if you don't slow down."

🎧 143

He was right, of course. If you don't take the time to look, you'll never manage to see anything. I picked up another album and forced myself to go ❻more deliberately. I paid closer attention to details, took note of ❼shifts in the weather, watched for ❽the changing angles of light as the seasons advanced. Eventually, I was able to detect subtle differences in the traffic flow, to ❾anticipate the rhythm of the different days (the ❿commotion of workday mornings, ⓫the relative stillness of weekends, the contrast between Saturdays and Sundays). And then, little by little, I began to recognize the faces of the people in the background, the ⓬passers-by on their way to work, the same people in the same spot every morning, living an instant of their lives in the ⓭field of Auggie's camera.

🎧 144

⓮Once I got to know them, I began to study their ⓯postures, ⓰the way they carried themselves from one morning to the next, trying to discover their moods from ⓱these surface indications, as if

---

❶an unrelenting delirium of redundant images: ★前項⓾ と同じような表現で、「重複する写像の、容赦ない狂乱」が直訳。　❷in feigned appreciation: さもわかったような顔をして　❸seemed unperturbed: 落ち着き払っているように見えた　❹a broad smile: 満面の笑み　❺You'll never get it: わかりっこない　❻more deliberately: もっと慎重に　❼shifts in the weather: 天気の細かい変化　❽the changing angles of light: 日々変わっていく光の角度　❾anticipate: 〜を予想する　❿commotion: あわただしさ、喧噪　⓫the relative stillness:（平日

る。重複する写像が、容赦なく、幻覚のように押し寄せてくる。言うべき言葉も思いつかないので、私はなおもページをめくりつづけながら、さもわかったような顔でうなずいていた。オーギー本人はといえば、いっこうにそわそわする様子もなく、満面に笑みを浮かべて私を眺めている。が、写真を見はじめて何分か経った時点で、彼は突然口をはさんだ。「それじゃ速すぎる。もっとゆっくり見なくちゃわからんよ」

　たしかにそのとおりだ。じっくり時間をかけて見るのでなければ、何も見えてはこない。私はもう一冊のアルバムを手に取り、もっと丹念に進むよう自分に言い聞かせた。細部にもっと注意を払い、気候の変化にも留意し、季節が移るにつれて光の角度が変わっていく様子にも気をつけた。するとじきに、車の流れの微妙な違いがわかるようになり、一日一日のリズムのようなもの（平日の朝の喧噪、それに較べての週末の静けさ、土曜と日曜のあいだの対照）も予測できるようになった。やがて、少しずつ、背景にいる人々の顔が見分けられるようになった。勤め先へ向かう通行人たち。毎朝同じ人が同じ場所を通って、オーギーのカメラの視野のなかで、それぞれの人生の一瞬を生きている。

　人々の区別がつくようになると、つぎに私は、彼らの姿勢に注目した。毎朝の彼らの歩きぶりを吟味し、表に現われた特徴から、その胸のうちを推し測ろうとした。私はだんだん、自分が彼らの物語を想像でき

のあわただしさと較べての）静かさ　⓬ passers-by: 通行人 ★passer-byの複数形。　⓭ field: 視野　⓮ Once I got to know them: ひとたび彼らのことを知るようになると　★get toは「〜するようになる」。　⓯ postures: 姿勢　⓰ the way they carried themselves: 彼らの歩き方　⓱ these surface indications: こうした表面的な徴候

I could imagine stories for them, as if I could ❶penetrate the invisible dramas locked inside their bodies. I picked up another album. I was no longer bored, no longer puzzled as I had been at first. Auggie was photographing time, I realized, both natural time and human time, and he was doing it by planting himself in one tiny corner of the world and ❷willing it to be his own, by ❸standing guard in the space he had chosen for himself. As he watched me ❹pore over his work, Auggie continued to smile with pleasure. Then, almost as if he had been reading my thoughts, he began to recite a line from Shakespeare. ❺"Tomorrow and tomorrow and tomorrow," he muttered under his breath, "time creeps on its petty pace." I understood then that he knew exactly what he was doing.

🎧 145

That was more than two thousand pictures ago. Since that day, Auggie and I have discussed his work many times, but it was only last week that I learned how he acquired his camera and started taking pictures ❻in the first place. That was the subject of the story he told me, and I'm ❼still struggling to make sense of it.

🎧 146

Earlier that same week, a man from the *New York Times* called me and asked if I would be willing to write a short story that would appear in the paper on Christmas morning. My first impulse was to say no, but the man was very charming and persistent, and by the end of the conversation I told him I would give it a try. The mo-

---

❶penetrate: 〜を見通す　❷will(ing) it to be his own: 意志の力でそれをわがものにしようと努める　❸stand(ing) guard: 護衛する、番をする　❹pore over . . .: 〜にじっくり見入る　❺"Tomorrow and tomorrow and tomorrow . . . on its petty pace.": 明日、また明日、明日、時は小きざみな足どりで一日一日を歩む　★シェークスピア『マクベス』第5幕5場を踏まえた言葉。シェークスピアでは"Tomorrow, and tomorrow, and tomorrow,/Creeps in this petty pace from day to day . . ."となっている。　❻in the first place: そもそも　❼still struggling to make

るような気になっていった。彼らの肉体のなかにとじ込められた、見えないドラマに到達できるような気になっていった。私はもう一冊のアルバムを手に取った。もはや退屈ではなかった。もう最初のようにとまどってはいなかった。私にはわかったのだ。オーギーは時間を撮っているのである。自然の時間、人間の時間、その両方を。世界のちっぽけな一隅にわが身を据え、それをわがものにすべく自分の意志を注ぎ込むことによって。みずから選びとった空間で、見張りに立ちつづけることによって。作品に見入っている私を眺めながら、オーギーは相変わらず、上機嫌ににこにこ笑っている。と、まるで私の思考の流れをさっきからずっと読みとっていたかのように、彼はシェークスピアの一節を暗唱しはじめた。「明日、また明日、また明日」と彼は呟くように言った。「時は小きざみな足どりで一日一日を歩む」。そう、自分がやっていることの意味を、オーギーは完璧に把握しているのだ。

　それ以来、すでに二千枚以上の写真が撮られた。オーギーと私は、あの日以来何度も、彼の作品について話しあってきた。けれども、そもそも彼がどういういきさつでカメラを手に入れ、写真を撮るようになったのか、それを知ったのはつい先週のことである。彼がしてくれた話というのが、まさにそのことをテーマにしていたのだ。そして私の方は、その話の意味を捉えようと、いまも頭をひねっている最中なのである。

　先週のはじめに、ニューヨーク・タイムズの記者が私に電話をかけてきて、クリスマスの朝刊に載せる短篇を書かないかと言ってきた。私は最初、特に考えもせずに断わったのだが、その記者というのがなかなか感じのいい男で、しかも粘り強かった。かくして、会話が終わった時点で、私はその男に、とにかくやってみます、と返事をしてしまっていた。

sense of it: その意味を理解しようといまだ頭をひねっている

ment I hung up the phone, however, I fell into a deep panic. What did I know about Christmas? I asked myself. What did I know about ❶writing short stories on commission?

🎧 147

I spent the next several days in despair, ❷warring with the ghosts of Dickens, O. Henry and other masters of the Yuletide spirit. The very phrase "Christmas story" had unpleasant associations for me, evoking dreadful outpourings of hypocritical mush and treacle. Even at their best, Christmas stories ❸were no more than wish-fulfillment dreams, fairy tales for adults, and ❹I'd be damned if I'd ever allowed myself to write something like that. And yet, how could anyone propose to write an unsentimental Christmas story? It was ❺a contradiction in terms, an impossibility, an ❻out-and-out conundrum. ❼One might just as well try to imagine a racehorse without legs, or a sparrow without wings.

🎧 148

❽I got nowhere. On Thursday I went out for a long walk, hoping the air would clear my head. Just past noon, I stopped in at the cigar store ❾to replenish my supply, and there was Auggie, standing behind the counter as always. ❿He asked me how I was. Without really meaning to, I found myself unburdening my troubles to him. "A Christmas story?" he said after I had finished. "Is that all? If you buy me lunch, my friend, I'll tell you the best Christmas story you

---

❶ writing short stories on commission: 依頼を受けて短篇を書く　★アメリカの作家は、特定の雑誌に原稿依頼を受けて書くことは少なく、書き上げた作品を作家のエージェントが方々の雑誌に送って掲載を乞うというやり方をとることが多い。　❷ warring with the ghosts of Dickens, O. Henry and other masters of the Yuletide spirit: ディケンズ、O・ヘンリーをはじめとする、クリスマス気分の巨匠たち　★ディケンズは『クリスマス・カロル』が、O・ヘンリーは「賢者の贈り物」がそれぞれ有名。Yuletideはクリスマスの季節のこと（Yuleはキリスト降臨祭）。　❸ were no more than

電話を切ったとたん、私は激しいパニックに陥った。クリスマスについて、いったい私に何がわかるというのか？　そもそも、注文に合わせて短篇を書くなんていう仕事について、私に何がわかるというのか？

　その後の数日を、私は絶望に包まれて過ごした。ディケンズ、O・ヘンリ、その他もろもろの、キリスト生誕の日をめぐる作品を残した先達たちの幽霊と格闘を続けながら。そもそも私にとっては、「クリスマス・ストーリー」という言葉そのものが不快な連想を伴っている。お涙頂戴の、甘ったるい、嘘でかためた代物があふれ出てくる感じ。どんなによくできた作品でも、クリスマス・ストーリーとはしょせん、願望充足の絵空事、大人のためのおとぎ話にすぎない。そんな話を自分が書くなんて、冗談じゃない。といって、センチメンタルでないクリスマス・ストーリーを書こうなどと思う人間がどこにいるだろう？　そんなものは自己矛盾である。とうていありえない、掛け値なしの自家撞着である。脚のない競走馬、羽根のない雀を想像する方が、まだしも楽というものだ。

　仕事はいっこうに進まなかった。木曜日になり、外気に触れて頭をすっきりさせようと、私は長い散歩に出かけた。ちょうど正午を過ぎたあたりに、葉巻を補充しに葉巻店に立ち寄った。いつものように、オーギーがカウンターの向こうに立っている。どうだい、元気かい、と彼は私に訊いた。べつにそういうつもりはなかったのだが、気がつくと私は、自分の悩みをオーギーに向かって洗いざらい打ち明けていた。「クリスマス・ストーリー？」私が話し終えると彼は言った。「それだけのことかい？　だったら俺に昼飯をおごってくれたらさ、わが友よ、あんたに最高のクリスマス・ストーリーを聞かせてやるよ。それも、隅から

---

wish-fulfillment dreams: 願望充足の夢にすぎない　❹I'd be damned if . . .: 〜するなんて冗談じゃない　❺a contradiction in terms: 名辞矛盾　★決まり文句で、"married bachelor"（既婚の独身者）のような矛盾を含んだ表現のこと。　❻out-and-out conundrum: まったくの謎　❼One might just as well try to . . .: 〜するのと似たようなものだ　❽I got nowhere: いっこうに進まなかった　❾to replenish my supply: ストックを補充しに　❿He asked me how I was: ★要するに"How are you?"と訊いただけであって、べつに悩みを打ち明けるようもちかけたわけではない。

ever heard. And I guarantee that every word of it is true."

🎧 149

　We walked down the block to Jack's, ❶a cramped and boisterous delicatessen with good pastrami sandwiches and photographs of ❷old Dodgers teams hanging on the walls. We found a table at the back, ordered our food, and then Auggie ❸launched into his story.

🎧 150

　"It was the summer of ❹seventy-two," he said. "A kid came in one morning and started stealing things from the store. He must have been about nineteen or twenty, and I don't think I've ever seen a more ❺pathetic shoplifter in my life. He's standing by the rack of paperbacks along the far wall and ❻stuffing books into the pockets of his raincoat. It was crowded around the counter just then, so I didn't see him at first. But once I ❼noticed what he was up to, I started to shout. He ❽took off like a jackrabbit, and by the time I managed to get out from behind the counter, he was already ❾tearing down Atlantic Avenue. I chased after him for about ❿half a block, and then I gave up. He'd dropped something ⓫along the way, and since I didn't feel like running anymore, I bent down to see what it was.

🎧 151

　"It turned out to be his wallet. There wasn't any money inside, but his driver's license was there along with three or four snapshots. I suppose I ⓬could have called the cops and had him arrested. I had

---

❶a cramped and boisterous delicatessen: 狭苦しく騒々しいデリカテッセン　★デリカテッセンはサンドイッチなどを食べさせる簡単な食堂。　❷old Dodgers teams:★「かつてのドジャース」というのは一九五七年を最後にドジャースがブルックリンからロサンゼルスに本拠地を移してしまったため。　❸launched into his story: 物語を語り出した　❹seventy-two: 一九七二年　❺(a) pathetic shoplifter: 情けないくらい下手な万引き　❻stuff(ing): 詰め込む　❼noticed what he was up to: 奴が何をやっているかに気づいた　★up to にはいろいろな意味があるが、ここでは「(何

隅まで実話って保証つきのやつだ」

　我々は店を出て、ジャックスに出かけていった。ジャックスは狭苦しく騒々しい食堂で、パストラミサンドが美味く、昔のドジャースの写真が壁に並んでいる店である。我々は奥の方のテーブルに座って、食事を注文した。それから、オーギーが物語を語りはじめたのである。

　「七二年の夏だった」と彼は言った。「ある朝、一人の小僧が店に入ってきて、品物をかっぱらいはじめたんだ。歳は十九か、二十ってとこだな。とにかく、あんなに下手くそな万引きは見たことないね。店の手前の壁ぎわに置いた、ペーパーバックのラックの前に立ってさ、レインコートのポケットに片っ端から本をつっ込んでるんだ。ちょうどその時はカウンターのまわりに客が大勢いたんで、俺もすぐには気がつかなかった。でも、万引きだ、とわかったとたん、俺は大声でわめいたね。そしたら奴は、脱兎のごとく逃げ出した。俺がようようカウンターから出たころには、もうアトランティック・アベニューをすたこら走ってた。俺は半ブロックくらい追いかけて、それであきらめた。小僧の奴、逃げる途中で何か落としていってね。俺ももうそれ以上走る気がしなかったから、何だろうと思って、しゃがんで見てみた。

　それは小僧の財布だった。金は一銭も入ってなかったが、運転免許証と、写真が三、四枚あった。こっちがその気になれば、警察に電話して、奴を逮捕させることもできたろうな。免許証に名前も住所も書いてある

his name and address from the license, but I ❶felt kind of sorry for him. He was just ❷a measly little punk, and once I looked at those pictures in his wallet, I ❸couldn't bring myself to feel very angry at him. Robert Goodwin. That was his name. In one of the pictures, I remember, he was standing with his arm around his mother or grandmother. In another one, he was sitting there at age nine or ten dressed in a baseball uniform with a big smile on his face. ❹I just didn't have the heart. He was probably ❺on dope now, I figured. A poor kid from Brooklyn ❻without much going for him, and ❼who cared about a couple of ❽trashy paperbacks anyway?

🎧 152

"So I ❾held onto the wallet. Every once in a while ❿I'd get a little urge to send it back to him, but I kept delaying and never did anything about it. ⓫Then Christmas rolls around and I'm ⓬stuck with nothing to do. The boss usually invites me over to his house to spend the day, but that year he and his family were down in Florida visiting relatives. So I'm sitting in my apartment that morning feeling a little sorry for myself, and then I see Robert Goodwin's wallet lying on a shelf in the kitchen. I figure ⓭what the hell, why not do something nice ⓮for once, and I put on my coat and go out to return the wallet ⓯in person.

🎧 153

"The address was over in Boerum Hill, somewhere in the ⓰projects. It was freezing out that day, and I remember getting lost a few

---

❶felt kind of sorry: ちょっと（kind of）気の毒になった　★kind of はこのように形容詞にかかることもあるし、動詞にかかることもある。*e.g. I kind of like it.*　❷a measly little punk: しけた不良のガキ　❸couldn't bring myself to feel very angry: あまり怒る気になれなかった　❹I just didn't have the heart: とてもその気になれなかった　❺on dope: ドラッグをやっている　❻without much going for him: 先行きろくな見込みもない　❼who cared about...?: 〜なんてどうだっていいじゃないか？　❽trashy: クズみたいな　❾held onto...: 〜をそのまま持っていた

んだからね。でも俺は、その小僧が何となく可哀想に思えたんだよ。どうせそこらのケチな不良なわけだろ、写真を見てるうちに、怒る気も失せちまってさ。ロバート・グッドウィン。それがそいつの名前だった。一枚の写真では、たしかそいつが、お袋さんだか祖母(ばぁ)さんだかの肩に腕をまわして立っていた。べつの写真では、九つか十のころのそいつが、野球のユニホームを着て、にこにこ笑って写ってた。とてもじゃないけど、気の毒でね。いまじゃおおかたドラッグ漬けになっちまってるんだろうし。ブルックリンの貧乏人の家に育って、先の見通しだって明るいわけない。アホなペーパーバック二冊や三冊、どうだっていいじゃないか？

　というわけで、俺はその財布を手元に置いといた。ときどき、小僧に送り返してやろうかなっていう気になることもあったけど、結局ずるずる何もしなかった。そうこうするうちに、クリスマスが来た。ところが俺は何もすることがない。いつもなら店のオーナーが家に呼んでくれるんだが、その年は家族を連れてフロリダの親戚のところに出かけちまったんだ。それで俺は、クリスマスの朝だってのに、アパートでぶらぶらしてた。そのうちに何だか、自分が哀れになってきてね。で、ふっと台所の棚を見ると、ロバート・グッドウィンの財布がそこにある。そこで俺は考えた。ま、この際だ、たまにはいいことをしようじゃないか、とね。それでコートを着て、財布を返しに出かけた。

　住所はボーラム・ヒルと書いてあった。団地が並んでるあたりだよ。凍てつくように寒い日だってのに、めざす建物が見つかるまでに何度も

---

⑩ I'd get a little urge to . . .: 〜しなくちゃという気に少しなるのだった　⑪ Then Christmas rolls around: ★語りが現在形になったのは、物語世界にすっかり入り込んでいる感じ。　⑫ stuck with nothing to do: 何もすることがないまま身動きがとれない　⑬ what the hell: ★「ええい、こうなりゃ」という感じ。　⑭ for once: たまには　⑮ in person: 自分で　⑯ projects: 団地

times trying to find the right building. Everything looks the same in that place, and you keep going over the same ground thinking you're somewhere else. Anyway, I finally get to the apartment I'm looking for and ring the bell. Nothing happens. I assume no one's there, but I try again ❶just to make sure. I wait a little longer, and just when I'm about to give up, I hear someone ❷shuffling to the door. An old woman's voice asks ❸who's there, and I say I'm looking for Robert Goodwin. 'Is that you, Robert?' the old woman says, and then she ❹undoes about fifteen locks and opens the door.

🎧154

"She has to be at least eighty, maybe ninety years old, and the first thing I notice about her is that she's blind. 'I knew you'd come, Robert,' she says. 'I knew you wouldn't forget your ❺Granny Ethel on Christmas.' And then she opens her arms as if she's about to hug me.

🎧155

"I didn't have much time to think, ❻you understand. I had to say something ❼real fast, and ❽before I knew what was happening, I could hear the words coming out of my mouth. 'That's right, Granny Ethel,' I said. 'I came back to see you on Christmas.' Don't ask me why I did it. I don't have any idea. Maybe I didn't want to disappoint her ❾or something, I don't know. ❿It just came out that

---

❶just to make sure: 念のため　❷shuffling to the door: ★shuffle は、足を引きずるようにして歩くこと。　❸who's there: どなたです　❹undo(es): (鍵を) 外す　❺Granny: お祖母ちゃん　❻you understand: わかるだろ　❼real fast: ★アメリカ英語では、形容詞や副詞を修飾するときに really の代わりに real を使うのは会話では普通。　❽before I knew what was happening: 自分でも何がなんだかよくわからないまま　❾or something: ★日本語の、ほとんど意味のない「とか」に近い。　❿It just came out that way: ただそういうふうに言葉が出てきた

迷子になった。ああいう団地って、何もかもおんなじに見えるんだよな。違う場所に出たと思っても、実は同じところをぐるぐる回ってたりする。まあとにかく、やっとのことで目当てのドアにたどり着いて、呼び鈴を押した。反応なし。留守かな、とも思ったけど、念のためってこともあるから、もういっぺん押してみた。しばらく待ってみて、やっぱり駄目かと思った矢先に、誰かがのそのそドアの前にやって来るのが聞こえる。年寄りの女の声で、どなたです、って訊くから、ロバート・グッドウィンを探してるんです、と答えた。『お前かい、ロバートや？』と婆さんは言った。そして、十五はあるんじゃないかっていう鍵を一つずつ外して、ドアを開けてくれた。

　この婆さん、どう見ても八十は行ってたね。ひょっとして九十に届いてるかな、っていうくらいださ。で、まず気がついたのは、婆さんの目が見えないってことだった。『きっと来てくれると思ってたよ、ロバートや』と婆さんは言った。『わかってたんだよ、お前がクリスマスの日にエセル祖母ちゃんを忘れるわけないもの』。そして婆さんは、俺を抱きしめようとするみたいに、両腕を広げた。

　俺にはゆっくり考える時間はなかった。わかるだろ、とにかくとっさに何か言わなきゃならない。で、自分でも何がなんだかよくわからないうちに、言葉が勝手に口から飛び出していたんだ。『そうだとも、エセル祖母ちゃん』と俺は言った。『クリスマスだもの、祖母ちゃんに会いに帰ってきたんだよ』。何でそんなこと言ったんだ、なんて訊かれても困る。俺だって見当もつかないもの。ひょっとして、年寄りをがっかりさせちゃ悪いとか、そんなふうに思ったのかもしれん。どうなんだろうな。とにかくそういうふうになっちまったんだよ。もう次は、婆さんが

way, and then this old woman was suddenly hugging me there in front of the door, and I was hugging her back.

🎧 156

"I didn't exactly say that I was her grandson. ❶Not in so many words, at least, but that was the ❷implication. I wasn't trying to ❸trick her, though. It was like a game we'd both decided to play—without having to discuss the rules. I mean, that woman *knew* I wasn't her grandson Robert. She was old and ❹dotty, but she ❺wasn't so far gone that she couldn't tell the difference between a stranger and her own ❻flesh and blood. But it made her happy to pretend, and since I had nothing better to do anyway, I was happy to ❼go along with her.

🎧 157

"So we went into the apartment and spent the day together. The place was ❽a real dump, I might add, but what else can you expect from a blind woman, who does her own housekeeping? Every time she asked me a question about how I was, I would lie to her. I told her I'd found a good job working in a cigar store, I told her I was about to get married, I told her a hundred pretty stories, and ❾she made like she believed every one of them. 'That's fine, Robert,' she would say, nodding her head and smiling. 'I always knew things would ❿work out for you.'

---

❶Not in so many words, at least: 少なくともはっきりそう言葉に出して言ったわけじゃない ★ in so many wordsは「はっきりと、あからさまに」の意味の決まり文句。 ❷implication: 言外の意味 ❸trick: 〜をだます ❹dotty: ぼけた ❺wasn't so far gone that she couldn't . . .: 〜できないほどぼけちゃいなかった ❻flesh and blood: 肉親、身内 ❼go along with her: 話を合わせる ❽a real dump: ものすごく汚い場所 ❾she made like . . .: ★=she acted as if . . . ❿work out: うまくいく

その場で俺をひしと抱きしめる、俺も婆さんを抱き返す、てな具合になっていた。
　俺はべつに、自分がその婆さんの孫だってはっきり認めたわけじゃないぜ。少なくとも、言葉に出して、そうだよ、俺はあんたの孫だよ、なんて言っちゃいない。まあ何となくそういう雰囲気はあったけどな。といって、婆さんをだます気でいたわけでもない。言ってみりゃ、俺たち二人でゲームをやることに決めたみたいなものさ ―― ちゃんとルールまで相談したわけじゃないけどね。つまりだな、婆さんだって、俺が孫のロバートじゃないってことくらい、ちゃんとわかってたんだよ。そりゃあ相当な歳だし、けっこうボケてもいる。だけど、赤の他人と肉親が区別できないほどボケちゃいなかったよ。要するに、孫が来てるふりをするのが楽しかったんだな。となれば、俺だってどうせほかにすることもない。いいでしょう、そういうことならこっちも話を合わせましょう、そう思ったわけだよ。
　というわけで、俺たちはなかに入って、その日一日を一緒に過ごした。こう言っちゃ何だけど、とにかくおそろしく汚ないとこでね。ま、向こうは目の見えない婆さんの一人暮らしだ、きちんと掃除しとけったって無理な相談だよな。こっちの近況を婆さんにあれこれ訊かれるたびに、俺は嘘をでっち上げた。うん、葉巻の店に職が見つかってね、いい仕事だよ。うん、今度結婚することになったんだ。とかなんとか綺麗ごとを並べたら、向こうも全部信じてるふりしてさ、『よかったねえ、ロバート』って言うんだ。うんうんうなずいて、にこにこ笑って。『わかってたんだよ、お前のことだもの、きっといつかうまく行くはずだって』。

🎧 **158**

"After a while, I started getting pretty hungry. There didn't seem to be much food in the house, so I went out to a store in the neighborhood and ❶brought back a mess of stuff. A ❷precooked chicken, vegetable soup, a bucket of potato salad, a chocolate cake, all kinds of things. Ethel had a couple of bottles of wine ❸stashed in her bedroom, and so between us we managed to put together a fairly decent Christmas dinner. We both got a little ❹tipsy from the wine, I remember, and after the meal was over we went out to sit in the living room, where the chairs were more comfortable. I had to ❺take a pee, so I ❻excused myself and went to the bathroom ❼down the hall. That's where things ❽took yet another turn. It was ❾ditsy enough doing my little ❿jig as Ethel's grandson, but what I did next was positively crazy, and I've never forgiven myself for it.

🎧 **159**

"I go into the bathroom, and ⓫stacked up against the wall next to the shower, I see a pile of six or seven cameras. Brand-new thirty-five-millimeter cameras, still in their boxes, top-quality merchandise. I figure this is the work of the real Robert, ⓬a storage place for one of his recent ⓭hauls. I've never taken a picture in my life, and I've certainly never stolen anything, but the moment I see those cameras sitting in the bathroom, I decide I want one of them for myself. ⓮Just like that. And ⓯without even stopping to think about it, I tuck one of the boxes under my arm and go back to the living

---

❶brought back a mess of stuff: いろいろ買って帰ってきた　❷precooked: 調理済みの　❸stash(ed): 隠しておく　❹tipsy: ほろ酔い気分の　❺take a pee: 小便する　❻excused myself: ちょっと失礼、と言った　❼down the hall: 廊下を通って　★downに上下の意味はない。　❽took yet another turn: さらに新たな展開が生じた　❾ditsy: ★=crazy　❿jig: 悪ふざけ、冗談　⓫stacked up against the wall: 壁ぎわに積み上げられて　⓬a storage place: 保管場所　⓭hauls: 獲物　⓮Just like that: あっさりと、何も考えずに　⓯without even stopping to think about it:

しばらくすると、俺は腹が減ってきた。家のなかにはろくに食べ物もなさそうだったから、近所の店に行って、食料を調達してきた。ローストチキン、野菜スープ、ポテトサラダ、チョコレートケーキ、何やかやと買い込んできた。婆さんはベッドルームにワインを二本ばかりしまい込んでて、結局けっこうまともなクリスマス・ディナーということに相成った。二人ともほろ酔い加減になってさ、食事が済むと、居間の方が椅子がいいっていうんで、そっちへ移ってどっかり座り込んだ。小便がしたくなったんで、俺はちょっと失礼と言って、廊下の先のトイレに行った。そこで話がまた変わったんだよ。婆さんの孫のふりをするってだけでも十分普通じゃないけど、つぎに俺がしでかしたことは、もうまるっきり狂気の沙汰だ。あんな真似を自分がやったことが、俺はいまだに許せない。

　俺はバスルームに入っていった。と、シャワーの横の壁に、カメラが六台か七台積み上げてあるじゃないか。新品の35ミリカメラが、箱に入ったまんま。とびっきりの高級品だ。ははあ、こりゃ本物のロバートの仕業だな、と俺は考えた。新しい獲物を、ひとまずここに隠しておくってわけか。俺は生まれてこのかた写真なんて撮ったことがなかったし、もちろん盗みを働いたことだってない。ところがだ、そのバスルームに積んであるカメラを見たとたん、俺は決めたんだ、こいつを一つ頂戴しよう、とね。一目見て、あっさりそう決めたんだ。それで、もう何

ちょっと待てよ、と考えたりもせず　★stop to ...は「～するために（いまやっていることを）やめる」。

room.

🎧 160

"I couldn't have been gone for more than a few minutes, but in that time Granny Ethel had fallen asleep in her chair. Too much Chianti, I suppose. I went into the kitchen to wash the dishes, and she ❶slept on through the whole racket, snoring like a baby. ❷There didn't seem to be any point in disturbing her, so I decided to leave. I couldn't even write her ❸a note to say good-bye, seeing that she was blind ❹and all, and so I just left. I put her grandson's wallet on the table, picked up the camera again, and walked out of the apartment. And that's the end of the story."

🎧 161

"Did you ever go back to see her?" I asked.

"Once," he said. "About three or four months later. I felt so bad about stealing the camera, I hadn't even used it yet. I finally made up my mind to return it, but Ethel wasn't there anymore. I don't know what happened to her, but someone else had moved into the apartment, and he couldn't tell me where she was."

"She probably died."

"Yeah, probably."

"Which means that she spent her last Christmas with you."

"I guess so. ❺I never thought of it that way."

🎧 162

"It was a good deed, Auggie. It was a nice thing you did for her."

---

❶ slept on through the whole racket: さんざん物音を立てても全然起きなかった　❷ There didn't seem to be any point in . . .: 〜しても仕方ないように思えた　❸ a note: 置き手紙　❹ and all: ★日本語の「とか」「だし」にも通じる、さして意味のない表現。　❺ I never thought of it that way: そういうふうに考えたことはなかった

も考えずに、カメラの箱を一つ脇に抱えて、居間に戻っていった。
　俺がトイレに行ってた時間は、三分にもならなかったと思う。でもそのあいだにエセル祖母ちゃんは、椅子に座ったまんま眠りこけてた。キャンティの飲み過ぎってわけだな。俺は台所に行って、皿を洗った。がしゃがしゃ音が立ったけど、婆さんはずっと、赤ん坊みたいにすうすう寝息を立ててる。わざわざ起こしたってしょうがない。そこで俺はもう帰ることにした。さよならってメモを残していくわけにもいかない。何しろ相手は目が見えないんだからね。だから、何もせずにあっさり立ち去った。婆さんの孫の財布をテーブルの上に置いて、カメラを抱えて、部屋から出ていった。それで話はおしまいだ」
「婆さんにはまた会いに行ったの？」と私は訊ねた。
「いっぺんだけ」とオーギーは言った。「三カ月か、四カ月経ってからだ。カメラを盗んだことで、自分でもすごく気分が悪かったんだ。だからまだ使ってもいなかった。で、ついに意を決して、返しにいったわけさ。でも婆さんはもうそこにいなかった。どうなったかはわからない。もう別の人間が越してきていて、訊いてみたけど、どこへ行ったか知らないって言われた」
「たぶん亡くなったんだね」
「ああ、たぶんな」
「ということはその婆さんは、最後のクリスマスをあんたと一緒に過ごしたわけだ」
「てことになるんだろうな。そういうふうに考えたことはなかったけど」
「いいことをしたじゃないか、オーギー。あんたは婆さんに、すごく

"I lied to her, and then I stole from her. I don't see how you can call that a good deed."

"You made her happy. And the camera was stolen anyway. ❶It's not as if the person you took it from really owned it."

❷"Anything for art, eh, Paul?"

"I wouldn't say that. But at least you've ❸put the camera to good use."

"And now you've got your Christmas story, don't you?"

"Yes," I said. "I suppose I do."

🎧163

I paused for a moment, studying Auggie as ❹a wicked grin spread across his face. I couldn't be sure, but the look in his eyes at that moment was so mysterious, ❺so fraught with the glow of some inner delight, that it suddenly occurred to me that he had made the whole thing up. I was about to ask him if he'd been ❻putting me on, but then I realized he would never tell. I had been tricked into believing him, and that was the only thing that mattered. As long as there's one person to believe it, there's no story that can't be true.

🎧164

"❼You're an ace, Auggie," I said. "Thanks for being so helpful."

"❽Any time," he answered, still looking at me with that ❾mania-

---

❶It's not as if the person you took it from really owned it: 君にそれを盗まれた人物だって、その本当の持ち主だったわけじゃあるまい ★It's not as if ... は「～というわけでもあるまいし」。*e.g. Why doesn't she buy us a drink? It isn't as if she had no money.*（酒の一杯くらいおごってくれたっていいじゃないか——一文なしってわけじゃあるまいに） ❷"Anything for art, eh, Paul?":「芸術のためなら何だって許されるってわけかい、ポール？」 ★作家である主人公にわざと自分自身の名前を与えて、現実と虚構との境界線をあいまいにしてしまうのは、いかにもオースターらしい手口。

いいことをしてやったんだよ」
「俺は婆さんに嘘をついた、婆さんのところにあった物を盗んだ。そんなののどこがいいことなのかね」
「婆さんに楽しい思いをさせてやったじゃないか。だいいち、カメラはもともと盗品だったんだろう。向こうだって本当の持ち主というわけじゃなし」
「芸術のためなら何でも許されるってやつかい、ポール?」
「そういうことじゃないよ。でもとにかく、あんたはカメラをちゃんと有効に使ってる」
「そしてこれで、あんたもクリスマス・ストーリーを手に入れた、だろ?」
「うん」と私は言った。「どうやらそうみたいだな」
　私はちょっと黙って、オーギーの顔に、いわくありげな笑みが広がっていくのを見つめた。たしかなことはわからない。でも、その瞬間彼の目に浮かんだ表情は、何とも意味深長に見えた。何かひそかな悦びをたたえて、ぎらぎら輝いているように見えた。私ははっとした。もしかしたら、何もかもオーギーのでっち上げじゃないだろうか? おい、僕をかついでるのか、そう問いつめてみようかとも思ったが、やめにした。どうせまともな答えが返ってくるはずはない。まんまと罠にはまった私が、彼の話を信じた —— 大切なのはそのことだけだ。誰か一人でも信じる人間がいるかぎり、本当でない物語などありはしないのだ。
「恩に着るよ、オーギー」と私は言った。「あんたは救いの神だ。本当にありがとう」
「お安いご用だって」と彼は私を見つめたまま言った。その目には、

実際、この短篇が『ニューヨーク・タイムズ』に掲載されたとき、事実と信じきって、「どうしてオーギーの写真を載せなかったのか」と投書してきた読者がたくさんいたという。　❸ put the camera to good use: カメラを有効に使う　❹ a wicked grin: いわくありげな (wicked) 笑み (grin)　★ grin はにっと歯が見えるように笑うこと。❺ so fraught with the glow of some inner delight: 何かひそやかな悦び (some inner delight) の発する光 (glow) をいっぱいにたたえて (so fraught)　❻ put(ting me) on: 〜をからかう、かつぐ　［以下❼〜❾脚注180ページ］

cal light in his eyes. "After all, if you can't share your secrets with your friends, ❶what kind of a friend are you?"

"❷I guess I owe you one."

"No you don't. ❸Just put it down the way I told it to you, and you don't owe me a thing."

"Except the lunch."

"That's right. Except the lunch."

I returned Auggie's smile with a smile of my own, and then I called out to the waiter and ❹asked for the check.

---

❼You're an ace: 君はいい奴だ　❽Any time: どういたしまして　❾maniacal: 躁病的な　★❹の wicked に通じる。［以上178～179ページ脚注］　❶what kind of a friend are you?: そんなの友だちとは言えんじゃないか　❷I guess I owe you one: じゃ僕は君にひとつ秘密の借りがあるわけだ＝じゃこっちもひとつ何か打ち明けなくちゃな　★one is a secret。　❸Just put it down the way I told it to you: 俺が話したとおりに書いてくれればそれでいい　❹asked for the check: 勘定してくれと頼んだ

AUGGIE WREN'S CHRISTMAS STORY by Paul Auster

相変わらずぎらぎらと狂気じみた光が浮かんでいる。「何てったって、秘密をわかちあえないようじゃ、友だちとは言えんだろ?」

「じゃこっちも何か打ち明けなくちゃな」

「いや、それには及ばん。いまの話を、俺があんたに喋ったとおりに書いてくれればいい。それで貸し借りなしだ」

「昼飯のおごりをべつにすればね」

「そのとおり。昼飯のおごりをべつにすれば」

 オーギーの笑顔に、私も笑顔を返した。そして私はウェイターに声をかけ、勘定にしてくれと頼んだ。

Authors & Translator

バリー・ユアグロー
1949年南アフリカ生まれ。59年にアメリカ移住。『一人の男が飛行機から飛び降りる』(*A Man Jumps out of an Airplane*, 1984:邦訳96年)や本書掲載「ハッピー・バースデイ」収載の『たちの悪い話』(*NASTYbook*, 2005:邦訳07年)など、奇抜な設定でありながら、ときに愉快でときに悲しい、妙な現実味を感じさせる短篇を得意とする。

——

レベッカ・ブラウン
1956年カリフォルニア州生まれ。本書掲載作を収録した『私たちがやったこと』(*Annie Oakley's Girl*, 1993:邦訳2002年)をはじめとして「幻想レズビアン小説作家」(柴田)とでも呼ぶべき作風の作品が多い。『体の贈り物』(*The Gifts of the Body*, 1995:邦訳2001年)、『家庭の医学』(邦訳2002年)など死をリアリズムで描いた作品もある。

——

ケリー・リンク
1969年フロリダ州生まれ。95年にデビュー後、世界幻想文学大賞(「スペシャリストの帽子」99年)やネビュラ賞(「ルイーズのゴースト」2001年)などさまざまな文学賞を受賞。本書掲載作のようにゾンビを登場させるというシュールな設定ながら、リアルな日常的情景を描く絶妙なセンスを持つ。夫と出版社スモール・ビア・プレスを共同経営している。

——

スチュアート・ダイベック
1942年イリノイ州生まれ。『シカゴ育ち』(*The Coast of Chicago*, 1990)、『僕はマゼランと旅した』(*I Sailed with Magellan*, 2003)といった、生まれ育った50年代のシカゴの下町を舞台にした連作短篇を発表。本書掲載作「ペット・ミルク」をはじめとして、すぐれた短篇に贈られるO・ヘンリー賞を4度受賞している。

——

スティーヴン・ミルハウザー
1943年ニューヨーク州生まれ。本書掲載作収録の『イン・ザ・ペニー・アーケード』(*In the Penny Arcade*, 1986)、表題作でO・ヘンリー賞を受賞した『ナイフ投げ師』(*The Knife Thrower*, 1998年)など、現代アメリカでは稀な耽美的・ロマン主義的な作風で知られる。子供と芸術家を主人公に据えた物語が多い。大学で教鞭も執っている。

——

ポール・オースター
1947年ニュージャージー州生まれ。1985年から86年にかけて発表した、ニューヨークを舞台とした作品をまとめた「ニューヨーク三部作」で高く評価される。本書掲載作にインスピレーションを得た映画監督ウェイン・ワンが手がけた『スモーク』や、自身でも監督した『ルル・オン・ザ・ブリッジ』など映画との関わりも深い。

——

柴田元幸
1954年東京都生まれ。東京大学名誉教授。著書に『翻訳教室』『アメリカン・ナルシス』『ケンブリッジ・サーカス』、村上春樹との共著に『本当の翻訳の話をしよう』などがある。本書掲載の作家以外にも、スティーヴ・エリクソン(『ゼロヴィル』)、マーク・トウェイン(『ハックルベリー・フィンの冒けん』)、ジャック・ロンドン(『火を熾す』)など、現代・古典の多数の作家作品を翻訳。雑誌『MONKEY』責任編集。

Acknowledgements

HAPPY BIRTHDAY by Barry Yourgrau
Copyright © 2005 by Barry Yourgrau
Permission for this edition was arranged through The English Agency (Japan) Ltd. Reprinted by permission of Barry Yourgrau c/o Writers House LLC
『新潮』(2005年9月号)にて柴田訳初出／『たちの悪い話』(新潮社)所収

FOLIE A DEUX by Rebecca Brown
© 1993 by Rebecca Brown
Japanese/English anthology and English straight reading rights arranged directly with the author through Tuttle-Mori Agency, Inc., Tokyo
『小説 トリッパー』(1998年冬季号)にて柴田訳初出／『むずかしい愛』(朝日新聞社、1989)、『私たちがやったこと』(マガジンハウス)所収

THE GREAT DIVORCE by Kelly Link
© Kelly Link 2005
Japanese/English anthology and English straight reading rights arranged with Kelly Link c/o Massie & McQuilkin c/o The Fielding Agency, LLC, Beverly Hills, California through Tuttle-Mori Agency, Inc., Tokyo
『新潮』(2005年9月号)にて柴田訳初出／『マジック・フォー・ビギナーズ』(早川書房)所収

PET MILK by Stuart Dybek
Copyright © 1984 by Stuart Dybek
Permission for this edition was arranged through The English Agency (Japan) Ltd. Reprinted by permission of Stuart Dybek c/o ICM Partners acting in association with Curtis Brown Group Limited.
『シカゴ育ち』(白水社、1992)にて柴田訳初出／白水Uブックス所収

SNOWMEN by Steven Millhauser
Copyright © 2011 by Steven Millhauser
Japanese/English anthology and English straight reading rights arranged with Steven Millhauser c/o ICM Partners, New York acting in association with Curtis Brown Group Ltd., London through Tuttle-Mori Agency, Inc., Tokyo
『イン・ザ・ペニー・アーケード』(白水社、1990)にて柴田訳初出／白水Uブックス所収

AUGGIE WREN'S CHRISTMAS STORY by Paul Auster
© 1990, Paul Auster
Japanese/English anthology and English straight reading rights arranged with Paul Auster c/o Carol Mann Literary Agency, New York through Tuttle-Mori Agency, Inc., Tokyo
© 2004, NPR®, Audio was originally broadcast on NPR's All Things Considered® on December 25, 2004, and is used with the permission of NPR. Any unauthorized duplication is strictly prohibited.
『Literary Switch』3号(1991年11月)にて柴田訳初出／『スモーク&ブルー・イン・ザ・フェイス』(新潮文庫、1995)、『翻訳夜話』(文春新書)所収

新装版
柴田元幸ハイブ・リット

2019 年 12 月 13 日　初版発行

著者・朗読者：バリー・ユアグロー／レベッカ・ブラウン／ケリー・リンク
　　　　　　　スチュアート・ダイベック／スティーヴン・ミルハウザー／ポール・オースター
編訳者：柴田元幸
編集：株式会社アルク 出版編集部
AD：松田行正＋杉本聖士
発行人：田中伸明
英文校正：Peter Branscombe
協力：佐伯弘美（朗読コーディネート）
DTP：株式会社秀文社
印刷所：シナノ印刷株式会社

発行所：株式会社アルク
〒 102-0073　東京都千代田区九段北 4-2-6　市ヶ谷ビル
TEL：03-3556-5501
FAX：03-3556-1370
Email：csss@alc.co.jp
Website：https://www.alc.co.jp/

・落丁本、乱丁本は弊社にてお取り換えいたしております。
・アルクお客様センター（電話：03-3556-5501　受付時間：平日 9 時〜 17 時）までご相談ください。
・本書の全部または一部の無断転載を禁じます。
・著作権法上で認められた場合を除いて、本書からのコピーを禁じます。
・定価はカバーに表示してあります。
・ご購入いただいた書籍の最新サポート情報は、以下の「製品サポート」ページでご提供いたします。
　製品サポート：https://www.alc.co.jp/usersupport/
・とくに断りのない限り、本書に掲載の情報は 2019 年 12 月現在のものです。

Printed in Japan © Barry Yourgrau, Rebecca Brown, Kelly Link,
Stuart Dybek, Steven Millhauser, Paul Auster, and Motoyuki Shibata

PC：7019059　ISBN：978-4-7574-3386-1　C0098